Mingle All the Way

J.P. Sterling

Mingle All the Way

© copyright 2023 J.P. Sterling

Editors: Rebecca Carpender and Brenda Bastien

Proofreader: Samantha Pottie

Contents

One
Jade O'lette

Schreeeeeech. Schreeeeeech.

Yanking the covers over my head so hard that I almost disjointed my shoulder, I held my breath and tuned into the I'm-clearly-a-ghost-scratching sound outside my bedroom window. My lungs screamed for oxygen, and I inhaled a deep breath of stale hot air. Suddenly, the discounted price on my new rental house made *so* much more sense. I had suspected something like this since it was an older neighborhood. Not only a little old, but we're talking colonial times. That's what the realtor called this house. A colonial. All I saw was thirteen hundred dollars a month rent in a city where nothing was under two thousand. I signed on the line so fast that I practically left a smoke trail behind my pen.

This was my year of saving money, as I did whatever I could to cut corners. If I did the mathing correctly, at the end of next year I could pay off all my debt. All my student loans, plus the credit card debt I had acquired after unexpectedly losing my middle-school teaching job last spring. Having been locked into my old rental agreement and without a job, I drained every penny out of my savings, and then some. I did what I could to honor the contract, but even though I eventually found a job as a barista, I didn't make the same money as I had teaching. I fell further behind every month. Or at least until I found this budget rental at the exact time my previous rental contract expired.

Speaking of the discounted house, this was my first night in the house, and I'm not sure I signed up for a ghost. Unless he was like Casper, who transforms into a hot date for the dance. Christmas was around the corner, and I could use an escort for my work Christmas party.

"I'm beautiful, strong and brave," I whispered. It sounded dumb, but I had listened to this podcast where the dude said to repeat what you want to be. I'd been doing it for almost a year now, and bad things kept happening. It clearly wasn't working, but I was terrified of stopping. *What if it got worse?* "Oh, and rich," I added.

Schreeeeeech.

"I heard you!" I forced a brave voice as I peeled back my blanket, peeking out. "I know you're here, but I'm trying to sleep. You can cut it out now."

Schreeeeeech.

Tapping my finger to my chin, I mused. He's clearly a male ghost because he's pretending not to hear me.

Maybe I'll have a closer look.

I eased one foot off the bed, softly hitting the bare wood floor, and gently shifted my weight onto that leg, careful to not make a peep. Not sure why I was worried about disturbing mister-clamorous-hot-invisible dude when he obviously wasn't worried about *his* noise level.

Casing the four hundred square foot studio apartment, which was my part of the house, for a weapon, I settled on the broom stowed in the closet. Now to make my legs carry me across the room. I eased one foot before the other, tiptoeing across the squeaky wood floor. I opened the closet door, and my gaze unexpectedly landed on a pair of over-sized, glow-in-the-dark swimming goggles.

You never know . . .

Without a second thought, I tugged the goggles over my head, not taking the time to smooth out where the headband created a huge bubble of long dark hair above my head. I grabbed the broom, and a flashlight from the shelf, and Nancy Drew'd my way over to the window. I paused for a beat, swallowed the lump in my throat, and slowly exhaled. Breathing was so nice. Then I gradually peeled back the curtain . . .

Schreeeeeech.

"Ahh!" I jolted, my feet cementing to the floor in fright. My heart motored away, and even though I wasn't in danger, the moment's intensity left me lightheaded.

The neighbor's titanic tree branch dangled like creepy, giant fingers trying to claw into my room!

I breathed out a heavy release as the twiggy branch scraped against the metal siding until it thumbed off the side of the house.

A stupid branch! I held my chest, waiting for my heartbeat to slow.

A light switched on in the upstairs room in the house across the alley. Before I had time to think, a man stepped out on the upstairs veranda. He wore red flannel pajama pants and a white T-shirt. His hair was dark, with the perfect wave at the tips where it was slightly overgrown past his ears.

He was hot.

Somewhere in the universe, a calendar was missing their Mr. December.

My jaw fell. I could see him, but did that mean he could see me? I was standing here in my Christmas jammies and swimming goggles . . . I panicked and jerked the curtain closed. With a cringed expression on my face, I motored back to bed, yanking the covers tight around me, and rolled over on my side.

Now that I knew a ghost wasn't ready to wrap his fingers around my neck, I was finally ready to sleep.

Did Mr. December see me?

Nah, I'm sure he didn't.

The goggles. I forgotten I had them on, and they pinched the back of my neck. I started to yank them off, but my hair pulled with the elastic band. Wincing, I sucked in a hard breath. Get a grip, girl. I grabbed the front of googles and gave them an impatient tug over the back of my head. Now, I could finally rest. Squeezing my eyes shut, I tried not to think about the hunk across the alley, or how ridiculous I must have looked to him, no sir.

Schreeeeeech.

Two
Evan Gabbert

I had been watching my program when I heard a woman cry out, the shrill tone sent chills up my spine, and I leaped out of bed and fled to the veranda. The sea creature from the blue lagoon stared at me from the vacant apartment across the alley. I rubbed my eyes as I struggled to open them wider and took another step closer. "Ouch!" I slapped my mouth, suppressing my holler of pain. I had stubbed my toe on my other toe. Who does that? Apparently, I do.

Man, I need to lay off the Discovery Channel.

Or maybe it was the hot wings? I swiped my forehead with the back of my hand, checking for a fever. Serrano peppers always had that nightmares-and-night-sweats-cleansing effect on me.

No fever. I must be sleepwalking again.

I rubbed my eyes, trying to wipe my nightmare away, and when I reopened them, the creature was gone.

It worked.

"Evan!" My mom's "I'm-about-to-go-ginger" voice called up the stairs. Most people called the attitude of a redhead feisty. After having lived with a redhead a good portion of my life, I would say it's more special than that. "Ginger" deserved to be a verb. "Honey!" Her puffed curls crested the steps, and she emerged with Dolly, her hairless dog, cradled in her arms. "What in mistletoe mania are you screaming about? You scared Dolly half to death. I thought someone was breaking into the house."

I cocked my head to the side. "Scared?" My eyes landed on Dolly. She was wrapped in a hand-knitted baby blanket that matched her collar. Looking relaxed, her eyelids visibly drooped. She didn't look scared to me. This was obviously more about my mother. I stepped away from the window, my voice dropping into a mutter, "I, uh, thought I heard something and tripped on my foot."

"Evan." Her words came out smooth and empathetic. "This is not the first time you've woken up with these issues. You are spending far too much time watching those alien shows." She flicked her hand toward my TV, where it incriminatingly displayed *UFO Witness* paused on my big screen. "I'm worried about you. This isn't normal. You're in your thirties and living in your childhood home. Maybe I'm making this too easy for you—"

"Mom." This was her failure-to-launch speech, and I understood her plight. Still living at home, I was the nerd that the nerds made fun of, but I wasn't ashamed. I owned it.

It wasn't like I still lived in the basement and slept all day.

I recently moved *upstairs*.

I worked and paid rent.

I wasn't lazy.

I had lived on my own for most of my twenties. It was phenomenal, until I had one of those life-altering defining moments that made me hate corporate America, at the exact time my engagement to my ex-fiancée imploded. I pledged to put myself first, get out of the rat race and work for myself by opening my own computer repair shop. However, the first year was painfully slow, and I moved back home to make it work.

Living at home with parents was sort of a trend my generation was starting to normalize. Unless I wanted to have three side hustles and never sleep, I couldn't afford the cost of housing anymore. Long Island is one of the most expensive places to live. With my rent payment, Dad was able to work less overtime driving a city bus and finally save a little extra for retirement. I saw that as a win for all of us. Dad appreciated the money, but he never would admit that to my mom.

Not to mention, the extra money had improved my dad's health in more than one way. With his evenings free, he started walking. He lost a few pounds, which in turn helped his back. Mom began walking with him, and for the first time in a long time, they are enjoying each other, and I even see them holding hands.

"Please don't think I mind that you're here." She took a step forward, while rubbing Dolly under her chin. "But I worry that you're putting your life on hold because it's too easy here. Don't be afraid to make mistakes."

"Mom." I started but then halted as her eyes filled with tears of worry. She'd sacrificed so much for me. It wasn't worth arguing with her. Not in the middle of the night anyway, when we were both overtired. I pulled my lips into an understanding smile. "I appreciate your concern."

Her shoulders raised and lowered as she took a deep breath, cueing for her change of subject. "I forgot to mention I'm hosting an early Christmas dinner here, with your grandma and cousin Rob—"

I cut her off with a stern glare. I never wanted to hear a word about that jerk. Rob had always been the golden child in our family. It traced back to his mother being my grandmother's favorite, and my grandmother never bothered to hide her favoritism. When his parents died in a car accident, Grandma swooped in to raise Rob, and no matter how mean he was, Grandma put him on a golden pedestal.

Rob and I were only three weeks apart in age. When we turned eight, Grandma gave me a transformer, while Rob got a go-cart. When we got our driver's licenses, grandma let me pick her up and bought me lunch. Rob, on the other hand, got a new car.

Looking back, I understand my grandma was merely filling in for his parents, and my young brain never understood that. What still bothered me was Rob had made a game out of showing off the disparities. He got enjoyment from "winning" over me. I learned to ignore him, but ignoring my enemy turned out to be my biggest mistake, which still haunted me to this day.

You know the saying, "keep your friends close, but keep your enemies closer?"

He screwed me over in a way I could never forgive.

"I know what happened between you two," she said, shutting off my "I-hate-Rob" spiral. "I agree with you, it's best to avoid him. However, Rob specifically asked if you'd be here. He's flying in for just a few days. Maybe he wants to make amends? It would be nice if you could try to forgive him. After everything that's gone on in the world these last few years, maybe we could all get together for your grandma one more time. You know she isn't going to be around forever, and it means a lot to her. And it shouldn't be that bad. Maybe you can bring a date?" She held her hand out in pause, gesturing forward like I should get the hint, before she tacked on, "Maybe you should try a dating service to get you out of this rut? You never know."

I raised my eyes heavenward. She was giving up on me. Before I could stop my word fart, I blurted out, "I can bring a date. I have a girlfriend."

"Oh?" Her over-tweezed eyebrow quirked. "This is news to me."

"Yeah, we kept it quiet until we knew we were serious." My eyes didn't blink as I let out another lie. I was half amazed about how easy it was to lie, and half scared I had this amazing skill.

"You're serious?" Her voice turned up at the end into a happy squeal as she reached out and cupped my cheek with her palm, letting her hand linger while her smile grew, reflecting almost a giddiness. "I'm going to mind my own business, but I can't wait to meet her. Night, Evan." She backed out slowly, rubbing under Dolly's chin again, even though Dolly had nodded off already. Right before she exited, her eyes landed on my open laptop, seeing a half-completed application for an engineering job at NASA. Her eyes flashed to me, before slamming to the heavens. "NASA? How are you going to keep your girlfriend happy if you're up in orbit, pooping into a vacuum cleaner?" she muttered as she padded back down the hall. Her voice got even quieter, but I heard the faint, "Grandbabies, Evan, that's the goal, not the stinking moon. . ."

I wasn't slighted that she dissed NASA, because my mind was racing.

No, not racing. Crashing like a forty-two-car pileup, and I was in the center in a Ford Pinto!

What did I just do?

I slammed my hand to the side of my head, trying to stop the building pressure. Where was I going to find a girlfriend?

I couldn't back out now! My mom was so happy. She would be crushed. No, now I was committed to this. The thought of Rob coming here all smug. Clearly, he was coming here so I couldn't avoid him anymore, but I wasn't a fool. He'd be rubbing his perfect I-just-made-part-ner-at-my-law-firm life all up in my face.

Bringing a date would be mandatory if I wanted to sur-vive Rob's fat "I'm-winning" mouth, and it would also make my mom happy. The problem was I didn't know any available women. I worked alone at my own computer shop. In the summer, I'd go to the beach, but it wasn't exactly beach weather. Hence the Alien show marathon.

Where was I going to find a date in two days?

My eyes surveyed my room, landing on my collection of micro, self-built robots, all the way to my full-sized R2D2. Hmmm. I tapped my finger to chin. He might look cute with a wig. . .

Three

Jade

Late. Late. Late. No, not that kind of *late.* Trust me, these chocolate cravings told me I was right on time on that schedule. Oh, and the fact that I didn't have a husband and cute little house with a white picket fence assured me more. I was late for work. "Phew," I took deep breaths as I ran around searching for my boot. Dressed as an elf, I wanted my black boots to match my green dress. My boss, Portia, encouraged us to show our Christmas spirit. When I discovered the Christmas spirit made me extra tips, I was all in. I had quickly become obsessed with dressing in costumes.

How my boot had gone missing in the twelve hours I'd lived in this place, was a mystery I couldn't solve. I didn't even unpack, and here I was, losing stuff already. With no furniture except a bed, it couldn't get stuck under anything. Undoubtedly there must be a black hole in the apartment. It's not even an actual apartment, just a back room of this house remodeled into a studio. Everything is contained.

There's no place for footwear to hide!

Centering myself in the room, I turned in a circle, scanning the floor. Bed. Wall. Bathroom door. Another wall. Tiny kitchenette. Exit door. Bed again. No boot!

I scratched my head. Maybe it got sucked into a void?

I'd have to stop at the store on the way to work and grab a new pair. There was a Budget Shoes for Less across the street from my coffee shop. I'd used all my savings for the two- months' rent and security deposit on this apartment, and all I had was twenty dollars. Good thing today is payday. With my winter boots not an option, I slipped into the only other pair of shoes I had unpacked—my sandals. I threw one arm in my jacket, not wasting time to slip in my other arm, and hurried out the door.

Icy air slammed into my face, stealing my breath, and freezing dampness seeped through the slits of my sandals. If I wasn't having the best day before, all I could say was one word.

Snow.

So perfect. I forced my lips into a sarcastic grin and slid across sidewalk, toes stinging and red by the time I reached my car and grabbed for the door handle. Thankful to make it across without falling, I pulled on the handle and found it frozen stuck. I yanked more than a gentle tug, but nothing budged. I didn't have time for this! I grasped the handle with both hands, anchored one foot on my car, and pushed off, feeling the ice crackling. It was working!

I held my breath, and dug deep for one final heave, and at last, it flew open. I scurried inside with toes so numb I couldn't even feel the cold anymore. I really hoped for an upfront parking spot at the mall, or I'd risk frost bite with these temps. This was clearly some kind of torture. I started my car and waited for the engine to warm up. Not that I cared about engines, but that's what my Midwestern dad always told me to do.

After four minutes, my car still had its freezing vibrations thing going on, but I got impatient because I was going to be late. "Sorry, car," I breathed out. "I know you hate driving when you aren't warm, but I have to get to work." My toes were not even close to normal flesh toned when I applied my brake and shifted the gear into reverse, but I didn't have time to waste. I glanced over my shoulder, assessing my exit strategy. I had parked in the alley, where my landlord had told me to park, because the street had No Parking signs.

It was fine when I pulled in, but the neighbors across the alley had several cars, and they had crowded in, parking at weird angles. I cranked my wheel, ready to Houdini out of this parking situation. I pressed down on the gas, but the car didn't move. My tires spun. Clearly, I was on ice. I dug my teeth deep into my bottom lip, as this morning was overwhelming me. I put my car into drive and tried to pull forward, but my tires whirled again. I didn't even move an inch.

Okay. I blew out a frustrated breath, one that made my bottom lip flap. Then I put my car back into reverse and pressed harder on the accelerator.

Too hard!

The ice created a launch pad, and my car flew back, out of control. I "can't-handle-my-life" screamed and slammed on the brake. Unfortunately, the soles of my sandals were slick as snot. My foot glided right off the pedal, and I slammed into the neighbor's car!

Stunned, I stared forward, terrified to turn around. The car was obviously empty. At least I didn't have to worry about hurting anyone, but this was not good in so many ways. Due to my recent financial emergency, I had gotten behind on *all* my bills . . . including my car insurance.

It was first on my list to pay!

I even had the check made out, but it didn't change the fact it had lapsed over a month ago. A dollar could only go so far. If I didn't have it to spend, I couldn't poof it out of thin air. I took a deep breath, wriggled my toes, and stretched my neck. I was fine. And really, I wasn't going that fast. How bad could the damage be?

I was about to ease out of my car to assess the damage, when a guy with red flannel pants and white shirt came flying out of the neighbor's house. *What are the chances?* Blush crept up my cheeks and I facepalmed. The *same* Mr.

December who I saw last night. His dark brows furrowed tightly as he plowed through the snow. He was clearly enraged about me hitting his car.

This day—this month—this life—had been too much! I thought I had finally caught a break by finding this budget apartment. Evidently my bad-luck streak was never going to end.

Fanning my face with both hands, I struggled to cool the sting in my eyes.

"I'm beautiful, strong, and brave," I said out loud. Even though my brain told me not to say it, I added, "without car insurance."

I don't cry.

Unless I do.

I swallowed the lump in my throat and opened my car door.

Four

Evan

Five minutes earlier

Drawing my second spatula, I stood on guard like a knight in a duel as I slipped it under my jalapeno-and-cheese-six-egg omelet and carefully balanced it. The tension in the air was thick. I held my breath as I prepared for my double-spatula final flip. The capsaicin was pungent, wafting under my nose, making my mouth water. Just moments away from breakfast perfection. To complete this final spatula rotation, it would have to be quick and smooth. On three. One. I stepped closer to my pan, ensuring I was perfectly squared. Two. I swallowed and inhaled a deep breath. Ah. The fumes were so delicious. My tastebuds were begging for a taste.

Three . . .

BANG!

Startling, I dropped my spatulas, my omelet ripping as it cascaded down, and plopped right on top of my foot, sizzling on impact.

"Ahcha!" I yelled, as I kicked the smolder-ing-torch-of-deliciousness off and fought back tears of pain as my foot scorched crimson. I still didn't know what died outside, but with my injured foot, I was pretty sure I had *eggs*terminated all hope of ever winning the World Cup. Not that I played soccer, or even had a ball. My sport was surfing, but . . . I could have at least dreamed about playing soccer before this *egg*sult.

Forget soccer.

My foot blazed!

I ran-hopped out the backdoor, not stopping until I plunged my foot into the fresh snowbank. I was freezing, dancing in place, but my burned foot thanked me. I quick-ly packed the top of my foot with snow and pivoted to return inside when something appeared out of place . . .

"What the?" I called out, feeling the burn in my foot now fleeting to my chest. I instantly forgot about my foot and ran to my baby! A Chevy I hadn't seen before, had rear ended my classic Mustang. I slid over to the bumper, my anger was boiling over.

This was my *baby.*

The car I spent my high school years restoring with my dad. It was really the only time we had ever spent together, and so all of my memories of him were with this car. I never even drove it unless the weather was perfect. "What happened to you?" I asked my car in a voice filled with concern.

A shuffling noise pulled my gaze from my car and onto a lady with braided pigtails and brightly painted makeup, slowly pacing toward me, tears running down her face. Her arms wrapped across her chest protectively. When her eyes met mine, she seemed to struggle to hold my gaze because she kept blinking. As mad as I had been, my anger melted away because she looked so afraid. She bit her bottom lip and paused before finally speaking in a tiny voice. "Is this your car? Please don't call the cops."

My eyes slid back to my car. I built this car to be a tank. This elf had managed to hit my bumper perfectly, placing a nice dent in the center, but in reality, it was only a bumper. Nothing that couldn't be easily swapped out. Her car took the brunt of the damage, as her fender was smashed. I didn't want to tell her that's what Chevies do, but it made me smirk a little as I stood. Struggling to balance on my good foot, I said, "Ah, yeah." My eyes narrowed as my brain caught up. I'd never seen this woman here before, but clearly, she had moved into the apartment across the alley. Which meant that creature I had seen last night—yeah. My cheeks heated despite the icy air. Perhaps my mom had been right about me needing to cool off the alien shows?

"It is my baby—I mean car." Hating to see a woman cry, I kept my tone even. I definitely didn't want to be responsible for new tears. "It doesn't look *too* bad," I tacked on calmly, then nodded toward her car. "Your car is much worse. It's not even drivable."

Her eyes skirted to the fender, brows pulling up high, and her hand flew over her mouth, "Oh no!" she exclaimed. "That's not good."

I staggered forward and ran my hand over her wheel housing, confirming what I had thought. "All you need is a fender." I inspected the dent, pressing against the tire, which wasn't flat. "It should be easy to fix. Your insurance company might not even require more than one estimate for this because it's such a clean dent. You only need the one part—"

Her chin started to quiver, and new tears budded in her eyes.

I rushed to ask, "What did I say?"

Judging from the way she rapidly shook her head, I thought she was going to go into a hysterical wail. Instead, she said in a voice that was barely above a whisper, "I didn't pay my insurance bill."

"OOOh." I stretched out the word to sound like it had five syllables.

"I'm not a bad person," she swiftly continued. "I lost my teaching job, and everything piled up. I had to pay double the rent to get into this apartment. It was either put a roof over my head," she bobbed her head toward her car, "or *insurance*."

"Right." I wouldn't say I came from a place of extreme privilege, but I always had parents who had my back. Exhibit one: I was living with them. I wasn't in a place to judge her.

Her eyes were wide and vulnerable. She sounded as if she'd been down on her luck. My gaze paced back to my car, and it was . . . fixable.

Nothing I couldn't buff out.

I was also fairly handy, and in a position to help her. "Well, you can't drive your car like that." I pointed to the fender rubbing on the wheel. "I can pound this out for you, to make it drivable, but I would feel bad knowing you were still driving without insurance—"

"Are you calling the cops?" She sucked back a loud breath that sounded like a hiccup, but I gathered it was actually her fighting back new tears.

"No," I reassured her. "I'm going to help you. I'm not a mechanic, but I can replace a fender for you. I'm a bit of an inventor and know a guy who sells me used parts for things. I should be able to get you a deal on what you need, and I can fix it for you."

Her eyes paced over my face like she was lost and looking for a way out. "Why would you do that?"

Why would I do that? I mused, as I was happy to help her.

Here she was, just a single woman down on her luck.

Wait a moment . . .

Single?

She didn't have anyone to call to help her. So, that meant she had to be single. Right? If she'd had a boyfriend, she clearly would have called him to help her. She didn't call anyone. So, she was single. It was perfect math. A single woman was exactly what *I* needed. Maybe if I helped her, she could help me? It made sense enough to me to try. Not wanting to come on too strong, I tried to downplay my offer by tossing a shoulder up. "It looks like you need a break."

"I do." She exhaled slowly. In a calmer voice, she tacked on, "I get paid today."

I nodded, refocusing on how she was dressed as an elf. "Is there somewhere you need to be?"

Her inhalation was so loud I thought she was choking, but somehow, she wasn't, exclaiming, "I'm so late for work! I'm going to get fired." She spun on her heel as if she was going to run back to her driver's seat.

I called out, "If you give me a second to grab some shoes, I can give you a ride." Her eyes latched back on me as if she was checking to see if she had heard me correctly and I added, "I would feel better to see you get there safely."

"I hate that I have to accept your offer when you have already been way too nice to me." Her lips curled into an appreciative smile.

My pulse started to pound harder when I realized what was happening. I had literally been sent this perfect single woman gift at the exact moment I needed her. I tossed up a lazy one-shoulder shrug. "It's my day off, and it's my pleasure." I motioned to the Jeep, parked next to my Mustang. "Let's take my Jeep. It's my winter car. You can hop in, and I'll grab shoes and I'll be right back."

"Thank you." Her voice was so sweet, it made me pause and look back. In the commotion of everything, I hadn't noticed how pretty she was. Now that she wasn't crying, her eyes brightened, shining on me, making me feel good about being able to help her. It was Saturday anyway, and I had less than two days to find a girlfriend. She was obviously put here for a reason. I shrugged my shoulders, pulling up one side of my lips. "Don't mention it."

Five

Jade

With short winter days, it was already dark by the time I finished my shift. The air was crisp, but at least no new snow was forecasted. I stood outside the coffee house, a coffee cup in each hand, scanning the curb for my ride. The hot guy from next door had taken my number when he dropped me off at the shoe store this morning and made me promise to text him when I got off work. I insisted I could call an Uber, but he reminded me I was broke.

He instantly won that argument.

I wiggled my toes, feeling the squish in my new boots. I had found a pair on clearance that was a half size smaller than what I needed, but the price was in my budget. I had reasoned it would be fine. Not like I had to stand on my feet for an eight-hour shift or anything.

Since I was late for work, it had been only *seven* hours.

Clearly, my feet were fine*ish*.

And at least I still had a job. I was lucky because Portia, my nice manager, had been working. If it had been, Christian, the new owner, I don't think I'd have been so lucky.

A bell-ringing Santa stood next to me, shaking his bell. I avoided looking at him. However, it felt awkward, and I suspected he had telepathic powers that sensed the loose change in my coat pocket. I shimmied my drinks into one hand and dug in my pocket, pulling out some lint and the forty-seven cents I had gotten as change from the shoe store.

Holding my cinched fist up, I scooted over to the bucket, and fed the coins one by one. Santa, who looked nothing like classic Santa, donned purple dreadlocks hanging out of the bottom of his backwards ball cap and a pierced lip. He smiled at me with even teeth peeking out. "What's your Christmas wish?"

"Huh?" I blinked as his question sparked my focus on all my current issues and run of bad luck. "It depends. How many wishes do I get for forty-seven cents?"

He chuckled. Not the typical full belly roll you'd expect from Claus. It was more of a sarcastic smirk. "It's not the amount that matters." As I was about to stroll away, his gaze latched onto me, like he expected me to actually tell him my wish. I snickered dismissively but he continued to stare. "Oh! Um. Yeah. So since you're taking orders, and if the price is right, I want bad stuff to stop happening to me long enough to get caught up from the bad stuff that has already happened." I curled my lips into an uneasy smile. He didn't reciprocate the smile, so I figured I had asked for too much. "Okay, then." I sidestepped back to the curb, right as Evan rolled up in his Jeep.

I opened the door, and got in, taking a moment to notice he was dressed in jeans and a cotton zip hoodie. That was innocent enough, but it was the crooked smile on his face that stuck out the most. Even though I hadn't seen many of his smiles, something about the way it curled higher on one side told me he was up to something. I dug into my bottom lip with my teeth, fighting to keep a straight face while my nerves tugged in my gut.

Proceeding with an air of caution, I slid in next to him, handing over the extra cup of coffee. "I made coffee as a thank you. I wanted it to be a surprise, so I guessed at your order."

He quirked an eyebrow while staring at the cup, not daring to touch it. "Oh really?"

Sitting this close to this handsome man didn't make me nervous at all. Okay, maybe a tiny bit nervous. Definitely excited. "Yeah, when you work as a barista, you hone a talent for being able to tell people's coffee orders by how they are dressed."

"And my red flannel pants tipped you off?"

"Well, partly." I pushed the cup further in front of him. "Please, take this. I promise it's good." I was unsure of how much I wanted to disclose about my secret skills. He finally took the cup, and I explained, "The red flannel said you like cozy, so I assumed you preferred a hot drink. It's later in the day, so I went with decaf."

"I can live with that," he hummed out, his lips tight as if he was waiting to seal his approval.

"I didn't peg you for a chocolate guy. I went with a caramel macchiato because they make a nice dessert drink, and I figured you'd already eaten dinner."

He pushed his chin forward. "I'd say you got one of my top three favorites."

"See?" My smile grew as he took a sip, a pleased grin spread across his face. "What's your top favorite?"

"I actually prefer iced, but it's freezing out, so the hot coffee is nice." He took another sip before setting it in the cup holder. As he pulled the Jeep away from the curb, he flashed me a teasing smile as if he was purposely stalling. "Thank you. You didn't need to get me anything, but in case there's a next time, I love chocolate peanut butter frappes."

"Well, who doesn't like chocolate peanut butter?" I chortled. "But that's one of those drinks that's totally more dessert than coffee. I bet you think it's extra protein."

"It can be—"

"Nope," I popped the p. "We don't use real peanut butter. We use syrup, but a lot of people think it's healthier. Most coffee shops use syrup unless you pay extra." I relaxed in my seat. Evan headed into the intersection, but instead of taking a left to the freeway toward our homes, he went straight, leading out of town. "I knew you were a serial killer!" I blurted out.

"What?" He chuckled, flashing me a confused look, but instead of denying it, he played along, "How'd you figure it out so fast?"

"That's not the way to our houses." I gestured to the road, my smile seeding even more. After our award-winning embarrassing meeting this morning, I had no pressure to impress him because he'd already seen me at my worst. I only had up to go. I held up a detective finger. "You were too eager to give me a ride home. I figured something was up. You're taking me to your abandoned farmhouse with a secret underground chamber where you take all your victims."

He kept one hand on the wheel, continuing to watch the road, but snuck a glance at me. "You like horror movies, don't you?"

"Like them, hmm," I mused while pressing a finger to my lip. "I like to figure them out."

"Oh, you're one of those people who talk constantly while you watch them?" He shot me an accusing glare, but the smile on his lips told me he was still joking.

"I can be quiet." I sealed my lips tightly and turned to peer out my window, attempting to figure out where we were going. We were obviously in an industrial area of town that I'd never been in, and it was looking very deserted. "So, which movie are we doing today?"

He let out an easy laugh I was beginning to recognize. "None. We are going to see my friend, Rash. He sells used car parts and has a fender for you."

"Woo. Wait. What?" I blinked cautiously, my gaze slamming back to him. "You have a friend named Rash, and you say that like it's normal."

"It's not abnormal." He kept a straight face, but I gathered he was messing with me. Instead of being nervous, I bit back a smirk. This had to be one of the strangest two-minute conversations I'd had. We'd clearly skipped normal small talk, and somehow bounced town, hunting for a man named Rash. It should have felt foolish, but my mind ruminated on how he had spent his time searching for a cheap fender when he didn't even know me.

Plus, I was the one who crashed his car . . .

Who is this guy?

"Can I ask how much this fender is going to cost?" I asked in a serious tone, even though I really didn't want to know. Maybe I wanted to know a little. It was a bit like getting a Pap smear. Necessary to endure, but I mostly just wanted the uncomfortable part over. "I did get paid today, but in case you haven't figured it out, I'm what you call a nillionaire."

He chuckled his easy grin again. Now, I not only recognized it, but was beginning to enjoy it. "No money?"

I shot a finger gun at him. "Ding, ding, ding."

"I didn't ask about the money," Evan replied to my previous question. "Rash isn't much of a talker. He just told me to come on out." Evan turned onto a narrow road leading up to a small square house sitting next to a large industrial shop. With the only light coming from the glow of the TV from a darkened window, and a small house light above the shop, it was *extra* creepy dark. Evan slowed as he approached. The tires bouncing around the snow ruts were the only sound. To fill in the silence I whispered, "Why do I feel like this is a bad sequel to a series where I never watched the first movie, so I have no clue what's going on?"

Rash must have seen us approach as he was standing on his step—*with a saw*.

Swallowing, I was so out of my comfort zone, I sat stiffly, waiting for cues from Evan about what we would do next.

"Name that movie." Evan's smooth voice rolled out.

I pointed an accusing finger toward him. "Don't even."

Evan rolled down his window, and called out, "Hey, Rash. How's it going?"

Rash staggered up to the Jeep, nodding at each one of us. "Not bad." Other than the dark goatee that wrapped his mouth, he was bald, but he had kind eyes that he latched onto me. "You need a fender?"

"Yeah. I have a Cobalt," I squeaked out.

"That's your first problem." A smile crept on his lips, putting me a little more at ease as he leaned on the open window. "What year?"

"Ah, 2015."

"I got a fifteen." He ran a hand over his already smooth goatee. "If you got cash, I could do seventy-five bucks."

"Deal." I spurted back quickly before he changed his mind. The price was right but oddly, I felt like we were doing something illegal, which felt adventurous, and made excitement bubble in my chest.

"You guys can pull up next to the door." Rash motioned to the shop. "If you want to come in, you can, but there's no need." He flashed his hand saw at us. "It's still on the car, so it will take me a moment to grab it."

"We'll wait out here," Evan quickly agreed, and rolled up his window as he drove the Jeep forward. "Now that we know what movie this is, we might need some snacks."

I laughed inwardly, but not in an amused way. "I can't even think about it." Most of the mental tension which had built up all day was now released. This fender would cost me a fraction of what I had thought since Evan was fixing it for me. I still had no idea why he'd agreed to help me. I stared at Evan, feeling like I'd made a new friend. I wasn't sure how I'd ever repay him, but I would try. "I have no idea why you're helping me so much . . ." I paused for beat. "I'm sure you're busy, but if there is anything I can do for you, don't hesitate to ask."

His cheeks twitched, teasing he was going to say something. I was sitting so close to him that I could see a glimmer of something in his eye. My eyes narrowed, inspecting him. "There is something, isn't there?"

He blinked, but didn't pause. His words fell out in rapid fire, "I should keep my mouth shut because I don't want you to think I'm some weirdo."

"No," I pressed. "You dragged me out here to meet a guy named Rash, with a saw, and I haven't left yet. How much worse can it be?"

He let out a heavy sigh, that opened his thoughts to me. "So, you know how you didn't pay your insurance, but you were still driving, and that didn't make you a bad person?" He gestured toward me. "We're on the same page, right? I totally get you were in a bind."

"Right?" I scratched my chin, wondering where he was going with this. I hoped he wasn't still thinking about calling the cops . . .

"I'm sort of in a bind, too." He raked his hand through his hair and slid it down the back of his head until it hooked on his neck. "I could tell the truth to get out of it, or make something else up, but there's this guy who drives me crazy. It's my cousin, Rob, and he's coming over for Christmas dinner tomorrow." His face pinched like he was sucking on a sour lemon. "He is one of those cocky guys who always wins. And I hate that about him. And he has this fiancée, and I don't even have a girlfriend, but I accidentally told my mom I did, and before I could take it back, she told my grandma—"

My hand flew over my mouth, and I blurted out, "But you don't have a girlfriend!"

He tossed up a one-shoulder shrug. "Not unless you can count my life-size R2D2."

My volume ticked up a notch as if from the delight of cracking a mystery. "You want me to come over for dinner tomorrow and pretend we're dating."

"I mean . . ." He lifted his shoulders, holding them in pause. "Since you're right across the alley and can't dri-ve anywhere anyway—it makes sense." He dropped his shoulders, tilting his head toward me while he tacked on, "My mom makes awesome lasagna."

He was asking me out! My inner self turned a few amaz-ing cartwheels.

Not a real date. Now, I slumped in my seat.

But I didn't care about the logistics.

I hadn't been on a date in months, and he was asking me on a fake date! My heart pounded against my ribcage, and I quickly nodded with a full smile on my face. "I'll do it."

He gave me a suspicious side eye. "You will?"

"Yes." I held up my finger. Not in hesitation, but I was curious. "On one condition."

His expression deflated into a frown. It happened so suddenly, and he was overly animated about it, it made me want to laugh when he groaned out, "What's that?"

I did the gossip lean in. "Tell me, what's up?"

His brows furrowed down. "What do you mean what's up?"

"What's the deal with Rob? Why don't you have a girlfriend? You know, give me details." I left out the part about how he was obviously gorgeous. He should have women flocking to him. At least until they learned he lived with his parents, but I'm sure there had to be a reason for that. I was intrigued.

He made one of those coughs that sounded fake, but as his eyes almost bugged out of his head, I knew he wasn't choking. "Do you think it's that easy to summarize?"

"I don't think it's hard. I mean." –I gestured with to myself with both hands— "I don't have a boyfriend because I dated this guy for a year. We were the fun couple who always went out and met with friends. It was a total blast. When I lost my job, he ditched me because I wasn't *fun* anymore." My suppressed anger over my financial situation started to bubble up, so I quickly cut myself off. "That's my story." I pointed to him. "Now you go."

"He sounds like a total jerk." Evan's voice was softer, as he held my direct gaze a little longer than what would have been expected, before saying, "I'm sorry that happened to you."

"No big deal." I shrugged with my face. It probably would have needed to be over sooner or later. My unemployment helped me figure that out. I really couldn't care less about him. "It's your turn."

"I was engaged." His voice floated out as if the words were too sour to hold in his mouth.

"Woo. *Engaged*?" I tucked my leg up underneath me and pivoted in my seat to get a better look at him. "That's deeper than I thought. What happened?"

"Two years ago, I was doing everything my parents wanted me to do. I was living on my own, working at the big office corporate America gig, which I hated. And I was engaged to this girl I met at church. You know the story. It was like a movie." He flicked his hand out in a gesture. "She had the perfect family, and my parents were friends with her parents. We had chemistry together, so I asked her out. We hit it off, fell in love, and it was perfect. After we dated for a year, everyone kept asking when I would propose. I didn't think there was a rule that I had to set an expiration date on that sort of thing, but that's what everyone wanted from me, so I did."

His words fell away, and his facial expression was locked forward, as if he was concentrating on something outside the car, in the distance. He was quiet for a long time, I started to wonder if he forgot I was here. His Adam's apple bobbed before he finally continued, "I felt as if I was watching my life play out more than I was living it." He finally skirted his gaze back to me. "Have you ever felt like that?"

"Lately, I have been in survival mode, dodging one curve ball after the next. I don't feel like I'm watching, as much as I am reacting," I held an air of teasing in my voice, but he maintained his serious expression.

"Sometimes you don't know you're on the wrong path until something opens your eyes. For me, that something was as simple as finding an incriminating text message on her phone from my cousin Rob. I swore it was a joke that Rob had set up to get to me, but when I confronted her about it, she didn't deny she'd been seeing him."

"Oh." My lips made a perfect circle as I connected the dots. Evan's heartbreak of betrayal had to have been unbearable. I was oddly honored he was able to be this vulnerable with me. That had to be brutal to talk about. "No wonder you don't want him to win. He stole your fiancée. He's not a nice man."

"My ex." His lashes lowered back to his cup that he'd retrieved from the cup holder and picked at the edge of his lid for a long moment. "I have no idea why I told you that."

"Because I made you tell me why you didn't have a girlfriend," I quipped, then added in a forced cheerful tone, "I'll go to dinner tomorrow, and we'll totally show Mr. Not-so-Nice."

His eyes narrowed, skeptically. "Are you sure?"

"Yeah. Like you said, I can't drive anywhere anyway. Now I definitely want to help you show up your cousin." A loud pop sounded, causing us both to startle, and out of reflex, I grabbed the dash with my free hand. "What was that?"

"The shop door slamming." He motioned forward with his finger. "Rash is coming back."

"That didn't take long at all." I breathed a sigh of relief as I had almost completed the Saw encounter, and I hadn't even screamed. This day, that had started awful, kept getting better.

"No, it didn't." He opened his door, calling back. "You can stay inside. I'll load it in the trunk, and then I'll take you home."

"Thank you," I said, but I don't think he heard me as he had shut his door. I glanced in rearview mirror as he handed Rash some cash. I hadn't given Evan any money. Now, I'd have to pay him back. I was starting to feel like a burden with all these favors. Then I remembered our fake date tomorrow.

Goosebumps trickled down my spine.

It wasn't a real date . . . so I shouldn't be excited for real. Right?

Six

Evan

After busting out a couple of last-minute, run-ning-into-my-ex pull ups on my door frame, I dropped to the floor and opened the bi-fold closet doors. Scanning the pile of board shorts on one side and stretchy waist-band pants on the other, I got overwhelmed by my lack of options. I wasn't one of those guys you'd call fashion . . . whatever. I don't even know the word for a guy who cared about clothes. I liked comfort.

The knot in my gut told me tonight I needed to level up and wear dinner-appropriate pants. While I did have a pair of once-worn funeral pants, I avoided those like the plague. The doorbell rang and the bottom dropped out of my stomach. I was more nervous tonight than when I had an actual date. It had a little to do with Jade, as I hoped I didn't come off as some creep. She really did seem awfully sweet. However, most of my anxiety had to do with how I was lying to my entire family and hoped not to get caught.

Part of me couldn't believe I was attempting to pull off a fake date. Never in a million years had I thought I could find a date on such short notice. And then have her actually agree to this shenanigan. I still don't believe I asked. Before I knew what I was doing, the words tumbled out of my mouth. *She's the crazy one to agree to this!* Crazy, or maybe just fun? I rubbed the side of my recently shaved face. She seemed to be a fun-loving spirit who was willing to help, and I didn't hate the thought of spending time with her.

Maybe it would be fun?

Distant laughter cut through my concentration, cueing for the arrival of my cousin.

No, *not fun*.

Then, a softer giggle I had memorized followed.

Holly was here.

My heart was put in a chokehold.

I had clearly forgotten the effect Holly had on me.

How could she come to *my* house, with all *our* history? Never in a million years would I go anywhere to intentionally see her again. My mom wasn't one to meddle in my life, but it was out of character for her to go along with it. Even though a massive boundary had been crossed, I didn't blame my mom. This was clearly the finagling of Rob. He was up to something. How Holly went along with it was also beyond me. Evidently, Holly was as big a piece of work as Rob.

My eyes paced between the board shorts, and the stretchy pants as my adrenaline ramped up. "Whatever," I muttered as I pulled the funeral pants off the hanger and started to leave to shower. A niggling you-want-to-dominate voice in the back of my head piped up, and before I lost my nerve, I quickly turned back, snatching the matching funeral shirt, and tie. "This is unreal. I'm dressing up to eat in my own kitchen," I murmured while I crossed the hall to the bathroom.

"Evan!" My mom's perfect-hostess voice called from the bottom of the stairs. "Everyone is here."

I hollered down, "I'll be five minutes." I got into the shower as quickly as possible. It wasn't until I dropped the soap for the second time, I self-assessed something was up with my grip. It was undoubtedly medical because it wouldn't be anything else.

It clearly wasn't seeing Holly again for the first time in two years.

Or seeing Rob *with* Holly.

And it obviously had nothing to do with my fake date because . . . well, I was totally calm about that.

Okay, I was lying to myself, and it was D. All of the above.

By the time I dressed and successfully managed not to strangle myself with my tie, a cool sweat beaded down my lower back.

So much for the shower.

I slathered on another layer of deodorant and was about to call it good when the doorbell rang again. I bolted down the stairs as if taking hurdles, dodging my mom's poinsettia plants that were lined up, one on each step. Mom said the plants were festive. I referred to them as a fire hazard. Desperate for my mom—or anyone for that matter— not to get to Jade first, I flew to the foyer, slamming my entire body against the door just in time.

When I yanked open the door, I was instantly confused. The Jade I remembered wearing braided pigtails and painted rosy cheeks, wasn't here. This Jade had her hair down, pulled to the side, with soft waves and muted makeup that left me staring at her as if I was seeing her for the first time. Sure, I'd thought she was pretty before, but now she was stunning. Seeing her like this made me want to stand up taller and find random reasons to flex my biceps.

"Hey," her voice came out hushed and unsure.

"Hey . . ." I totally squeaked like a prepubescent boy on that one. Wincing, I inhaled deeply and tried again. "How are you?"

"Good," she quipped, gazing past me into the Christmas-cluttered foyer.

"G-Great." I stumbled over my fat tongue as I opened the door wider, now feeling like a complete tool because I'd clearly forgotten how to speak. "You can come inside."

"Is that Jade?" Mom's voice was noticeably closer, as she was already in the foyer. A dying-to-know smile was pinned on her face.

"Yes." I shimmied closer to Jade, not sure how to act. We hadn't discussed any ground rules, but I had to make this somewhat convincing. I put my arm around Jade's back, pulling her to my side. I prayed that she wouldn't slap me, but she didn't waste a beat, and slid her arm around me as well. A swirl of sweet vanilla, better than any frosting I'd ever smelled wafted under my nose. Obviously, it was Jade's perfume, but I had a hard time pretending not to notice. "This is my mother, Pearl—" My voice dropped off. Both Jade and my mom had gemstone names.

That was an odd coincidence that I'm sure had nothing to do with anything . . .

It's not like we were meant to be soulmates or anything.

My dad rounded the corner with an easy grin and waved toward Jade. I motioned to him. "My dad, Tony."

Dad was bald, thirty pounds overweight, and he had on his ugly Christmas Rudoph sweater he wore every year. Rudoph's nose lit up with an actual real Christmas bulb. The first year he had it, I was only ten years old, and it worked well, staying fully lit. Over the years, it must have developed a short in the wiring because now it would randomly blink, or go ominously dull at the most random times, like it was possessed. The thing used to give me nightmares as a child, and I can't understand why Mom hasn't "lost it" in the wash by now. He obviously still loved it, and true to fashion, Rudolph's nose creepily winked at Jade when Dad leaned in, shaking her hand. "Nice to meet you, Jade. Welcome to our home." I wasn't at all worried about Dad liking Jade or vice versa. My dad had practically earned a Ph. D in people skills for all the years he drove a city bus. He always put everyone at ease and could smooth out any turbulence.

"Thank you," Jade responded, standing a little stiffly with her eyes locked on Rudolph's creepy winking nose. This had to be awkward for her, and I vowed to do any-thing possible to help her feel comfortable. I was about to invite her further inside to take a seat, but something happened. I didn't even have to look; my body was so attuned to my ex's Holly's scent. Her smell was a tad spicy, like amber musk, instantly warming my lungs. Come to think of it, it was a great prelude to being stabbed in the back.

Holly had entered the room. I didn't think it was possi-ble for anyone to ever glow up more than she had already been. She was just one of those women born with a face of a seraphim, but I grinded my back teeth trying not to notice how huggable she looked in her cream sweater dress. Her turquoise eyes radiated with so much blue and green sparkle; you'd think you were lost at sea.

I wasn't playing my C game tonight. The only way to win was to pretend she didn't affect me. I planted my gaze on her and smiled as if I was on top of the world. "Holly." Her eyes were like a vortex that sucked me in, and I struggled to remember what I was supposed to be doing. Thankfully, Jade dug her fingers into my back, giving them a twisty squeeze, busting me out of the Holly vortex.

That was close. I shook off my tingles and I pointed out the rest of the crew. "This is Rob." I did a double take after barely looking at him the first time. Rob had a mustache. That was new. It made him look older. Furrier. Did Holly like that?

I tried not to stare, sweeping my gaze at my grandma, adding, "Grandma Clementine." Grandma leaned over her cane, peeking in from the other room as if coming all the way into the foyer was too much work. I doubted she could even see Jade since she was so nearsighted, she usually carried a magnifying glass in her apron pocket. I didn't blame her, though, we were extra crammed in this Christmas village foyer. I set my eyes back on Jade. She had a mischievous sparkle in her eyes, oddly putting me at ease. For the first time, I felt this could work. "Everyone, this is my girlfriend, Jade."

I had rehearsed this moment in my head so many times over the last twenty-four hours, but the way Jade Hallmark-movie smiled at everyone, and then latched her eyes back lovingly on me, beat anything I could have imagined. She was obviously playing to win, and a massive rush of relief rushed into my lungs.

My mom spoke waving her spatula in hand like it was traffic flags. "Dinner will be ready in a few minutes. Why don't you all have drinks in the living room and get to know one another."

Rob almost pounced on my mom. "I'll help you serve drinks, Pearl."

"Thank you, Robby." She called him by his childhood nickname and placed a hand on his shoulder, pausing in thought before motioning to the China cabinet in the adjacent living room. "Glasses are in there. The drinks are in the kitchen." Her inquiring eyes shot to me. "Evan, can you help Rob?"

"Suuuure," I called after my mom, who had already left the room with Rob on her heels. My dad and grandma wandered into the living room, and Holly was left standing next to Jade. I hated to leave Jade by herself with Holly. Not because I didn't think Jade could hold her own, but I was oddly feeling vulnerable with Holly so near me. I could handle Rob being Rob. That was a guy rivalry thing, but Holly . . . I breathed out, feeling the sweat build in the creases of my hands. If anyone could tell that Jade was a fake date, it'd be her. She knew me, and all my mannerisms more than anyone. I couldn't let her see she was having this effect on me. I leaned over and whispered in Jade's ear, "I guess I have to compete for best host with Rob. Are you okay talking to Holly?"

I thought she might snicker, but instead she threw her head back and laughed as if I'd said the funniest thing in the world. Out of the corner of my eye, I could see Holly watching us. Jade didn't take her eyes off me as she wrapped her other arm around me and drew me closer, bringing her lips to my ear, and whispering back, "Don't worry about me. I have seen this movie before. I know *exactly* what to do." Before she pulled away, she shocked me by pressing her lips to my earlobe for a quick in-Holly's-face nibble, and an electric shock jolted the side of my head, stunning me into a system malfunction.

I couldn't even turn my head. I was utterly immobilized!

She had a flirty we're-going-to-win smile on her face before she winked and took a few steps toward Holly. She quickly started a conversation by complimenting Holly's dress. Together they entered the living room, leaving me struggling to feel my face.

That was *not* what I had been expecting!

"Evan!" Mom called from the kitchen. "The wine is waiting for you."

I ran my hand along the side of my face, feeling it tingle as it slowly thawed. Then followed her voice to the kitchen.

Maybe this wasn't going to be so bad?

Rob cornered me by the island, with a glass in each hand. "Hey," his voice was hushed while his gaze was locked on the closed kitchen door. "I ah, wanted to bring something up while I had you alone."

I grabbed the closest wine bottle, and corkscrew, as I was anxious to do anything other than look at Rob's arrogant skinny face in my personal space. "Yeah," I muttered as if his mere presence was putting me to sleep.

"I know we had some issues in the past and all, but I was hoping we could put everything behind us. I ah, think things worked out for the better this way anyway. For both of us."

"You don't say." I jabbed the corkscrew in the cork and twisted it, funneling my frustration with Rob into each turn. I used all my strength to shove that thing deep into Rob—I mean, the bottle. Man that was satisfying.

"Yeah. I mean, you and Jade." He motioned to me, and then hooked his thumb back to himself, adding, "Me and Holly."

"Right." I gritted my teeth and yanked on the cork, pulling it out in one piece.

"I uh, wanted to come on this trip for one main reason." Rob shifted on his feet, leaning back on his heels as if he was pumping up his ego even more. "You know we got engaged, and I want to ask for your blessing. We are going to get married no matter what you say, but I don't want family gatherings to be awkward."

I lowered one eyelid, trying to calm the twitch that was starting to develop in my eye. It had to be because I was holding back my desire to slam my fist into his face, and it was building too much pressure. Now my ear was ringing because I clearly didn't hear him correctly. Did he just say he wanted my blessing? My anger boiled up my chest, and out my arm, triggering my fingers to curl into a fist. I'll give him a blessing—

"Boys!" My mom's cheery voice rang out. She had popped the top half of her body though the swinging kitchen door, appearing so joyful, even wearing her Christmas red lipstick, something she never did. She always said redheads can't wear red, but boy, did she look festive today. "What's the hold up on the drinks?"

I blinked once to refocus. Then added a second blink to shut off my anger. I couldn't do this to my mom. Rob wanted me to punch him to ruin my mom's dinner and make me look bad. This was a trap Rob had set to show the family I was the bully. I was on to him, and frankly over it. "I'm so over Holly, you can marry her in my living room for all I care." Jerking my head toward the door, I quickly filled the glasses with wine and said, "Let's go."

Seven

Jade

I led Holly to the plaid sofa next to the Christmas tree. It appeared Evan's mom still took the time to decorate the tree with the homemade ornaments from Evan's youth. My eyes caught an especially cute one, a paper stocking with cotton balls glued above his picture. He had a fun haircut with bangs in the front, and what looked like lightning bolts shaved into the near-buzzed sides. Clearly, he wore the getting-ready-to-rock-on look, and it was adorable.

I glanced back to Holly. If I'd met her on the street, I wouldn't have taken a second look, but everything about how she stared down her perfect nose at Evan, made me wish I had met her at work. I would totally pretend to spill iced coffee all over her. I couldn't imagine being in Evan's position and having to entertain his family with his cheating ex-fiancée.

I don't know why it bothered me so much.

Evan was hardly a friend, having known him for only two days, but he'd been extremely nice to me. I got the impression he was one of those nice guys who got walked on often. As I stared at Holly, I knew who'd done the walking.

Correction: traipsing.

"So . . . Holly." I flashed her more teeth than a smile. "I love your hair color. You must tell me your stylist's name. She did such a great job on your highlights." I bit back the part about how I could still tell she wasn't a natural blonde, but I didn't want to be a mean girl. That wasn't why I was here.

She stayed quiet, but smirked when Rob returned with two half-full glasses of red wine. He handed one to me first and passed the second one over to Holly while barely acknowledging her. He promptly squeezed between Holly and me, planting his gaze on me. "Tell us, how did you meet Evan?"

Evan appeared in the doorway with another wine glass, handing it to his grandma. His eyes locked on mine, and he nodded slightly as if yielding to me. "It's such a funny story, but actually, I crashed into his car." Running a hand through my hair, I tucked it behind my ear and pulled a bigger smile on my face. "It truly was fate stepping in, though, because ever since that happened, we've been inseparable."

Rob's eyes stayed dialed in on me. "And how long has that been?"

My eyes narrowed as his tone wasn't that sincere. I was careful not to name a time frame because I wasn't sure if Evan had given one. "A while."

"It doesn't matter." Evan swooped in, sitting next to me on the couch. Now we were all squished on the couch, sitting four people wide, with Rob and me still hip to hip in the middle. I leaned on Evan out of need for space and because I didn't want to feel Rob's boney hip. Evan tacked on, "I feel like we've known each other our whole lives, right Sugar Boo?"

He cringed as soon as the terrible nickname came out of his lips. I bit back my giggle by sipping my wine, with my shoulders noticeably shaking. Like he was trying to stifle me, Evan placed his hand on my knee. A shiver shot right through me, instantly melting all my humorous thoughts. Goosebumps traveled up my leg, and didn't stop until my cheeks flushed.

Yikes!

I took his hand into mine, lacing my fingers with his, and winked. "Right. Sugar Boo." I didn't feel like laughing anymore. Maybe I had been single way too long, but I hadn't ever experienced instant chemistry with someone just from them touching me.

Evan's grandma sat in an armchair near the stone fireplace and spoke in a voice that was deeper than what you'd expect for someone barely five feet tall. "Are you from here?" Her eyes locked on me. Everyone's eyes followed, including Evan's. Wow. I hadn't noticed how seriously dreamy his blue eyes were. Like right out of a photo-shopped magazine. "No." I wagged my head briefly, trying to pull my gaze away from Evan. "I actually grew up in the Midwest."

Rob leaned over, physically butting his perfectly aerodynamic face in. "I adore the Midwestern states. They are so wholesome. And how did you end up on the East coast?"

"Well." My gaze slid to the side, mentally retracing my life. "I graduated college with a degree in history, but no plan. I heard about the New York City teaching fellowships and applied." Although it was Rob who had asked the question, I shifted my gaze to Evan's grandmother, engaging her. "If you have a bachelor's degree, you can apply even if you don't have a teaching license. If you get accepted, you are hired to teach in an underserved public school while taking master's classes in education—"

"So, you're a teacher," Rob cut me off again. Even though he was sitting on the same couch I was, he stretched his neck as if he was hard of hearing and had a nosey-all-in-my-business expression that reminded me of a dog salivating. He clearly wasn't trying to hide the fact he was taking social scores.

"Er . . ." I bit my lip, pausing. I wasn't sure how much acting Evan wanted me to do. Was I supposed to make up a fabulous career or tell them the truth? The truth would be more believable. "I was," I affirmed before adding, "unfortunately, the district had cuts, so I was dismissed from the program before I could complete my master's degree. Without access to the program, my teacher's license is invalid. I'm taking some time to figure out my next career move right now." I rubbed my ear, pretending to adjust my earring. "I work at a coffee shop called Coffee Loft on Huntington Avenue at the moment."

"Coffee?" Rob's brows sprang up, his smirk seeding on his lips. "I served a lot of coffee in my internship days." He cackled as if he was competing in some annoying duck call contest. "Now that I'm a partner in my law firm, I won't be doing that anymore."

Evan squeezed my hand hard, sending me a be-tough signal.

I fought the urge to say something snarky. I was saved by Evan's mom calling from the kitchen, "Dinner is ready!"

Everyone filed into the kitchen, leaving Evan and me to loiter in the back. As we stood, he stayed in character by not dropping my hand. He leaned in, whispering in my ear, "You're doing great. Just one more hour."

I had half-forgotten I was only supposed to pretend to care about this interaction because it had somehow gotten personal. I wanted to wipe that smug grin off Rob's face.

Rob had become a weird placeholder for all the random people who'd been jerks to me in the last year. All the times I walked away and never had the chance to fight back.

I wasn't only fighting for Evan anymore.

This had gotten personal.

Eight

Evan

"If tomatoes are fruit." Jade set her fork down from her final bite of lasagna. "I'm voting ketchup and all tomato sauce in general are smoothies, which therefore means—"

"Don't even say ketchup is a healthy food," I placed my palm on the table between us, cutting her off with a teasing tone.

Pulling both perfectly groomed brows up defensively, she went on, "Who said that was what I was going to say? You wouldn't let me finish."

My grandma was chuckling, and even though she had her share of wrinkles, I could easily pick out her dimples. She was enjoying this way too much, so I gave her a playful glare. "Grandma, you cannot pick Jade's side on this. We are blood."

Jade and I had been bantering back and forth the whole meal. She was so witty. She had my parents and my grandma laughing the entire meal. Rob and Holly, who sat directly across from us, didn't say a word as they sullenly ate their food.

I had never seen my grandma so amused in my life. Grandma raised her hands like she was under arrest. "I never pick sides. I was merely laughing. Besides." Her lashes lowered, but they didn't completely conceal the humored sparkle in her pale blue eyes when she pretended to mutter. "Tomatoes are a vegetable."

"Oh!" Jade's jaw dropped all the way down. "You did not just say that."

Grandma tucked her bottom lip in, but it only fed her giant smirk. "They are a vegetable, or why would you put them in salad?"

"To make salad not toxic," Jade disputed, and the whole table, minus Rob and Holly, laughed.

Holly drained the last of her wine. As soon as her empty glass returned to the table, Rob retrieved the wine bottle and tipped it over to fill her glass. "Easy there," I teased Holly in the first direct comment I made to her all night. "We don't want a hair-holding situation again." Sitting next to Jade must have inflated my ego because I was never one to be confrontational. I held Holly's gaze as if I was daring her to remember our first meeting.

My parents had been bugging me to ask her out for months. When I saw her at a party, I started to pay attention to her. She wasn't much of a party girl. She quickly got ill, and all her friends ditched her. I found her on the deck, barfing over the railing, and made myself useful by holding her hair.

That's all I ever was to her . . . useful.

She used me until she ran out of uses.

Jade's hand randomly touching my thigh pulled me from my memory. She had an earth-to-Evan smile on her face, and she was laughing as she said, "I volunteered to help with dessert. Can you help with the cheesecake?"

I heard what she had asked, but I clearly wasn't functional. Her hand was still on my leg.

She should not be allowed to touch me without proper warning!

I wasn't emotionally immature or anything, but her touch was the antidote to Holly's memories. It set off a tsunami of shimmers that rocketed through my body, sending me back into failure-to-operate mode for the second time tonight. "Ch-cheese," I stuttered, still feeling the tingles resonate in my limbs. S-Sure." I slid from my chair, wholly shocked my legs could still do the leg thing. "I'll h-help you."

We ducked into the kitchen together, giggling like two partners in crime. As soon as the door was shut, Jade locked her eyes on me. "Boy, you got it *bad* for Holly. No wonder you had to deploy the fake date."

"What are you talking about?" I scoffed while I moved to the fridge, grabbed my mom's five-pound, cheery cheesecake, and set it on the counter.

"Your mom made that." Jade's eyes drifted to the cake as she thankfully dropped the previous topic. "That looks better than the ones we sell at the Coffee Loft. She should totally make these for us."

"You should tell her that." I grabbed the plates and forks and set them on the counter, while scanning the wall magnet for the perfect knife. "She's always wanted to have her own bakery."

"Tell her that?" Jade grabbed a fork and dug it right into the center of the cake. "I'll take orders."

I barely heard what she was saying because my eyes were locked on her fork sticking out of the center of the cake. "You can't eat out of the middle, you, you uncivilized person!"

She scraped off a layer of cherry filling and brought the fork to her mouth, clearly not sorry for ruining the cake.

"Who are you?" I kidded, pretending to be repulsed because I was actually disgusted, but didn't want to act like I was not cool. I slid the cake closer to me and positioned myself between the cake and her. "You can't eat the cake like that, you hog!"

"It's so good." She swiped the fork in her mouth. "You should try it."

"I'm going to try it like a normal person." I picked up the knife and sliced twelve perfect slices, making sure to keep the part Jade had eaten all on *her* slice. We had all the slices dished out on plates, lined up ready to serve.

And that's where it all went south.

I'm not a waiter. I should never be allowed to serve any food.

Lesson learned. I'll jot that down somewhere in my free time.

I tried to balance a plate on my arm like those fancy servers do, but it didn't even last three seconds before it flipped off my arm, plopping the cake down on the floor.

That should have been the end of it—but Jade . . . she wore a rascal smile, and she should clearly have taken all the blame. The spark was in her eye as soon as the cake splattered. She needle-nose-dolphin dove, swiping the biggest chuck right off the floor with her bare hands.

She was savage.

Also maybe a little unstable.

I didn't have to wait to see where this was going. This wasn't about a three-second rule. I'm no idiot. I grabbed a piece of cake from the counter and smooshed it into the side of her face while she struggled to get off the floor. She screamed, but her terror quickly transitioned to deep belly laughs which only set me off into the hugest rush of laughter I'd ever felt.

But I had an issue.

She wasn't done!

She grabbed my leg. That was her best defense. She was weak. Undoubtedly, she had no idea who she was up against. As she swiped the cake from her cheek, she tried to stand, but now the floor was slick, and she slipped. That didn't stop her from reaching all the way up and smashing a handful of cake right into my chest. "Stop!" I called between fits of laughter. "Truce. We must stop. People need to eat this cake."

She was finally able to find her footing, but she acted as if she didn't trust me when she took a stance against the wall, staring me down. "Truce?" she echoed.

"Yes." I motioned to the floor smeared in cheese and cherry filling. "My mom is going to kill you."

"Me?" She motioned to herself. With her plaster of cream cheese and cherry filling on the side of her head, she looked like she had been raised from the dead. I couldn't stop another fit of laughter.

Her eyes slid to the side. She was obviously trying to create a diversion as she planned her next attack. I wasn't letting her get away with that. I saw my chance, quickly swiping another slice from the counter. She was already running toward the exit. I was fast, grabbed her arm, pulling her back. I was *not* as smooth as I had planned because she slipped again. She dominoed me down with her, but not before she smashed the cake that I held right between us. She landed on top of me in the perfect little cheesecake human sandwich. She didn't move. Her dark hair cascaded down, framing her face.

I held my breath.

My heart motored rapidly from the laughter to the food fighting, and then there was the way her eyes hooked mine. Her eyes were kryptonite, blasting all memories I had ever had of Holly, and instantly filling that void with something I hadn't even seen coming.

"Evan!" My mom's voice sliced through the air like a hot knife on butter. "My cake!"

Jade's eyes bugged out of her head as she scampered to get off me. Humored tears ran down my face by the time I had finally managed to stand up, and then I saw them . . .

The cherry-on-top moment I couldn't have made up.

My whole family crowded at the door. They apparently had seen Jade and me lying on the floor together, rolling in cheesecake.

Grandma was almost choking with laughter. So was my dad. Holly was stoned-faced and backed out of the room with Rob on her heels.

When I locked my gaze back on Jade, she gazed at me as if we had suddenly created our own secret club. A world where only we understood the language, and everyone else didn't matter. Like a camera snapping a picture, my heart twisted as it captured this moment perfectly, saving it. I bit down on the side of my lip, as my heart continued to swell. Before I had a chance to rationalize it, I gave up. Jade was too powerful. This was the exact moment I started to fall for Jade.

Nine

Jade

"Did you see your mom's face?" I winced while ducking into Evan's Jeep, freshly changed into new jeans and an oversized comfy sweater. I took a moment to notice he had recently updated the air freshener in here, as Christmas tree pine smell permeated the air. It was festive, and I liked it. But it didn't do enough to wash away my guilt.

I had left the party right after the cheesecake brawl, because there was no way I could clean up without a shower. As soon as everyone else left, Evan texted me to meet him in his Jeep to get my car from his shop. "I could cry. She was so mad at me."

"She wasn't mad at you." He tilted his head to the side as if he was mulling something over. "Well, she was upset her cheesecake was ruined, but I told her what you said about selling them, and she was totally flattered. I think she'd be interested."

"Really." I pulled my door shut and buckled in, my nerves calming down. Not all the way down, but enough so I didn't hyperventilate. "Did she say so?"

"She didn't say it directly, but she's not the type to admit that. She's always been overly modest. Her cheeks got a little pink, and she started wiping the already spotless kitchen counters. That's what she does when she's wanting to overthink things."

I bit back a smirk, clearly seeing the path to make it up to her. "I will ask my boss tomorrow when I go to work."

Evan started the Jeep, letting it idle for a moment. "Are you ready to see your car?"

"Yeah, I am. I can't believe you fixed it already," I rambled into the change of subject. "That was amazing service."

Putting his car into gear, he backed out saying, "It wasn't a big deal."

I didn't realize prior to now, I had a thing for voices, and Evan's baritone voice made the tips of my lips turn up. It was unlike anything I had ever heard. I wouldn't call it raspy, but it had enough hoarse intonations that it was unlike anything I'd ever heard. I could easily listen to it for hours. I sighed, relaxing in my seat, when my memory pulled something up. "Oh." I held up my finger to interject in the silence. "I still have to repay you for the money you gave Rash."

"No." He shook his head admittedly. "Don't worry about it. You did an amazing job acting. I would pay a thousand dollars to see Holly and Rob's faces in the kitchen again . . ." His voice trailed off into a hearty laugh.

Even though I loved to see him happy, it stung a little. I went over there intending to play the role of the girlfriend. However, I didn't act. I was myself the entire time. He was still laughing as he turned the corner, and I added, "It was funny to see Rob. His face was so red. I felt sorry for Holly, though."

His brows bent down harshly, and he nearly shouted out in disgust, "Why?"

I tucked my hair back behind my ear as I thought about why, but I couldn't pinpoint it. "The look on her face wasn't shock like everyone else's. If I had to guess, I would think she still has feelings for you."

Evan threw his head back and guffawed, then rolled right into a chuckle. "Fat chance there. She burned that bridge a long time ago."

I wasn't convinced. I had been around plenty of mean girls in my life, and I recognized the look of jealousy. "How so?"

"She was my fiancée." His voice was filled with conviction as if he was going into battle. "I didn't easily let her go. I was a month away from saying vows to her. What kind of man would I be to give up? I had already made up my mind for better or worse with her. I reached out to her more than once, asking if there was something I did that made her cheat. She made it clear that she had zero feelings for me. It's hard to think about that now, but I didn't see it as dodging a bullet. I'm glad I'm not in that place anymore."

I bit down on my lip, running her expression over in my head. Something else was going on with her, but I couldn't place it. "Maybe she's jealous?"

Evan turned into an alley behind a brick building and killed the engine, completely ignoring my question. "Here we are."

"This is your shop?" I quickly unbuckled and jumped out of the Jeep.

"Not a shop." He waited for me at the door, and he punched numbers in the keypad. "It's a research lab."

"Oh." I pinned an amused expression on my lips, and we slipped through the door. At first glance, it looked like a two-stall garage, with my car in one bay, and stacked boxes along the wall in the other bay. There was a small bathroom in the corner, and a long worktable in the middle. Where it got interesting, was the row of life-sized robots standing in front of my car. "What are these?" I asked while slowing my steps.

"That's my research." He walked over to one and did some sort of weird sign language in front of it, and it immediately powered on. "This is Greta."

"Greta?" I stared at her, not sure if I should shake hands, she looked so real. "What kind of research?"

"It's always been my goal to work for NASA someday, but they've never asked me for an interview. So, in the meantime I've been experimenting with programming robots to do all sorts of fun things."

Planting a new smile on my lips, I was intrigued as this was not what I had expected to find from a thirty something who lived with his parents. "What kind of things?"

He wagged his head back and forth. "Here, Greta," he spoke to her slowly, "can you pick up my friend and put her on the chair?"

Greta swiveled without a sound and started rolling toward me. I took a giant step back. "No, don't pick me up." I shooed her away, but, before I knew it, she gently picked me up, squeezing her robot arms all the way around me like a clamp. The transition was relatively smooth, but I freaked out and tried to break my arms free. It didn't work, and she squeezed tighter. I stiffened and waited for her to glide to the chair. When she lowered her arms, they must have gotten jammed, because she didn't open her grasp. I was left levitating above the chair. "Ah, Evan," I squeaked out, my eyes on the chair, as I struggled to break out of her super huggie hold. It was no use. My arms were stuck. "How do I get her to let go without dropping me?"

"Greta," Evan cut in. "Let go of Jade."

"Security breached. Alarms engaged," Greta stated. "System shutting down."

"Don't shut down!" He yelled and slid in front of Greta, flinging the front control panel open, and hummed, "Hmmm, this isn't good."

"What's not good?" I tried to see what he was looking at, but Greta's hold on me was too strong. I couldn't bend forward at all.

"I'm not sure, but you must have resisted her enough for her to feel threatened. I've programmed her to shut down if she feels attacked."

"If she feels attacked?" I squawked, all the blood rushing out of my face leaving me dizzy. "What about me?"

His eyes locked on the exit. "I might have to pull up the code, but my laptop is at the house."

"Oh, no you don't!" I blurted out, before he had a chance to ditch me with Greta. "You are not leaving me."

"Ah, give me a sec." He got up, and ran into the other room, swiftly returning with a cord, and plugged it into his phone. "I might be able to do this on my phone."

"Can you just pull me out?" I waved my arms like I was drowning. My stomach quibbled. I didn't want to be stuck in this robot hold anymore.

"Well, I can try . . ." One side of lips curled up as if he was priming me for bad news. "She has been programmed to resist such things. She might let go, or she might squeeze you to death."

I stiffened, not even wanting to breathe now that I understood the severity of her sensitivity. "You're kidding, right?"

"Ha." His nervous sputter told me he wished he was. "Maybe we could trick her?"

"This isn't funny," I cried out, wondering if this was ever going to end, but now I was terrified to fight back.

"Relax, I have an idea." Evan's grabbed the other end of the cord and plugged it into Greta's back. "I think I can switch her to auto repair mode, and she should reset to baseline and let you out."

"Or?"

Evan didn't reply to my super-important inquiry. Instead, he hunched over his phone, typing in something I couldn't see. It was creepily quiet, as he worked, and I tried to ignore the sound of my panting. It was getting harder to breathe in this hold, and the harder I tried to stay calm, the quicker my breath ran in and out. "Ah, just another minute—" he muttered, as he moved to adjust something on Greta's back.

"System restore activated," Greta announced as she powered back to life, swiveled to face the opposite direction, raised both arms above her head—with me *still* in them—and opened her grasp. I was not prepared for the instant release, tumbling right out, but I was never happier to land flat on my face. I spread my arms out wide and gave it a nice hug.

"Wow. That was slick," I joshed, so glad to be out of her grasp. Not taking any chances on having her pick me back up, I army rolled to the side, fleeing far away from her, and scrambled to my feet, protectively backing up all the way against the wall. "I can see why NASA doesn't call," I said sarcastically, still panting to get my breath. Now that I was safe, I found the whole thing silly, and the release of adrenaline left me giggling.

"Yeah, we are still working on some things. I'm sorry about that." He flipped Greta's off switch again, and propped one hand on the wall next to me, leaning his weight on it casually. Never noticed before, but suddenly, I was an expert in leaning. He was great at it. He had this tilt in his gaze that made him even more intriguing. "We still have a long way to go but we'll get there."

"So, this is your job?" I tried to mimic his lean, but my arm was shorter, and it didn't have the same effect. Plus, my hand was sweating from being squeezed and began sliding up the wall, making me look super awkward. I quickly stood up straight, squaring my body with his. "I thought you installed Windows for people. You NASA science these robots?"

"That's my avenue. I do install Windows for some people. The laptop market is more lucrative than my mad scientist inventions. Some stuff pays the bills, and some stuff fuels my soul."

"I love that." My lips parted in awe as I could picture him spending long days, and even nights in here, getting lost in his element and having it out with Greta. Even though it had some glitches, it made me a little envious. I had a job, but I never had a thing that made me, me. I tried every hobby and sport, but I was never more than okay at anything. "I wish I had that."

"A mad scientist laboratory?"

"No, a passion that identifies me." I had my gaze locked on Greta. One part for security reasons. The other part, growing envious. "I never really had one thing."

"Maybe it's still coming," he said matter-of-factly as he opened a door that led into a retail space. Then he waved me forward. "Come on. I'll give you the rest of the tour."

"There's more?" I pretended to spin on my heel and head for the door, calling out. "Not a chance! I can't handle any more robots."

Before I took even a tiny step, he reached back and grabbed my arm, trapping me. An instant sonic boom exploded from his grasp and slammed into my heart. "No more robots. I promise."

I resisted staring at our hands because the physical explosion had been enough without me having to see it. Now, I was wishing I had a system restore button to reset my heart rate because something unnatural was happening. I couldn't ignore the pounding vibrations. Somehow—it was not luck, because I didn't have any of that—I managed to meander to a storefront, all the while I was still aware, okay, hyper focused, of the fact that he still held my hand. Maybe he'd forgotten he was holding it? Or forgot Rob wasn't here. I barely was able to pull my gaze away from him, to survey the store. It had normal computer displays and customer service areas. Everything was clean and modern. "This is very impressive," I managed to casually muster up. I hoped it was casual anyway.

"I don't know if I'd say it's impressive, but it does fill the space." He finally released my hand—to my huge disappointment, and he walked farther back into the hall to open another door, with stairs. "Up here is more storage, but you can follow me." He ascended the narrow stairs, speaking to me over his shoulder as I followed. "When I purchased this building, I had planned to remodel it into living quarters, but as you can tell," He flipped on a light switch, revealing open beams. "it has not gotten done yet."

Pacing forward, I took in the space. It was huge, with so much potential for a fantastic loft apartment. Spaces like these were a rare find. I knew that because I had spent months hunting for a nice apartment. He was sitting on the Bermuda triangle of available rental space. "Look at the view of the park!" I motioned out the large window at the literally picture-perfect overview of a small creek, and magnolia tree. "This is beautiful."

I felt him move in behind me. I didn't look back, but he was close enough I could feel the warmth of his body fill the air. Not sure why that made my toes curl under, but it didn't help when his voice came out softer than normal in his reply. "I thought so, too."

Dying to see his expression, I search for his face in reflection from the window. With his lips pinched tightly together, it didn't disappoint, as it clearly hinted, he wasn't telling me something. I was insanely curious to know more about him, pressing, "How come you never finished it?"

"I didn't decide not to." He sighed, not like he was giving up, but more like he was about to get transported into some sort of a dreamland. "It's still on my to-do list, it just fell to the bottom. I know I'm a little old to live with my parents, but things got complicated."

When I had first realized Evan lived with his parents, I had envisioned this dude who held down the couch all day next to two-day-old pizza boxes, but Evan wasn't like that at all.

He was sort of like me.

We were both trying the best we could.

He backed away from the window, and as he did my heart rate slowed to a more normal pace. When he nodded toward the stairs, he said, "I'll grab your keys. I know you said you have to work in the morning."

"I do." Reality slammed back into my brain, flashing a giant neon sign counting down the possible hours of sleep I could still get, and it wasn't enough. "I open at six."

"Ouch." Evan descended the stairs. "Sorry to keep you so late, but I figured you needed your wheels."

"It's okay. I haven't been sleeping well anyway. There's this branch. Actually—" I paused. "It's your mom's tree. It scratches on my window all night."

"That was totally you in the window the other night." He blurted out, his smile spreading across his face into a wonderful playful one. "I had convinced myself I had a nightmare. What was on your head?"

"Goggles. I was wearing my detective gear." I laughed because even though that was only two nights ago, it felt much longer than that, with so much happening since then. "I'm sure I looked like a nightmare."

We both chuckled, letting the incident go. I didn't need to explain myself. Perhaps it was because I'd already embarrassed myself so many times in front of him, he just understood me. It was a weird moment, where I felt like the easiness that we had when we hung out with each other was something special. Now we were downstairs, and he passed through the garage and pulled my keys off a hook, tossing them at me. I should have warned him never to throw stuff at me. Back to my thing about trying every sport and not finding one I was good at. I couldn't catch them, and they landed right by my feet.

"Sorry," Evan said, instantly leaning forward to retrieve them. "I should have given you a think fast."

"It's okay." I picked up the keyring before he could and fiddled with the ignition key.

"How come you're wearing sandals?" Evan's gaze was still on my feet. "It's like ten degrees outside?"

"It's dumb really." I gave him a dismissive wave, but I continued because we were at that point in our friendship where I was totally fine with making fun of myself. "I lost one of my winter boots. When I went to buy a new pair, they had the size six on sale. I didn't think a half size would make a big difference but after wearing them all night at your house, I needed to let my feet relax."

His head took a curious angle, and he was quiet for a moment before saying, "So . . . you met my family, you've seen my business, you even met my ex-fiancée and heard my whole dating history. Aside from the make and model of your car, I know nothing about you."

"That's not true," I took a defensive tone. "You know where I live." I held up a finger, popping up another finger each time I counted off something. "Where I work. I told you about my recent boyfriend. I think we're even."

"What about your family?" His chin moved forward, as if he was taking a stubborn stance. "You said they are in the Midwest?"

"Yeah." I pursed my lips out, thinking of something interesting to say but everything was pretty average. "Not much to tell there. Mom. Dad. Married. Like you, I'm an only child, so they weren't happy when I decided to move a thousand miles away. I think they are still waiting for me to fail, but they never say a disapproving thing. When I lost my fellowship, they pleaded with me to return. I don't feel like I fit in that small town anymore." I paused, remembering the blue-haired ladies who always gossiped at the diner. There wasn't anything terrible they'd ever said about me, but I felt gross knowing how much people talked in that town. "There's no sob story there. I was looking for a way out. Then I got laid off, but I like working at the coffee shop. It's nowhere near the stress of teaching. And it's crazy, now that I've decided I love dressing up in character every day, I'm fantastic at my job, and get amazing tips. The pay isn't that much less than teaching." I let my gaze fall on my fender. It appeared nothing had ever happened. "You did an awesome job." I quickly changed the subject, thankful to have it off of me. "Thank you."

His lips curled until the small lines by his eyes creased, and that's how I knew he was truly genuine. "You don't have to say thank you. I'm definitely the one who got the better deal." He chuckled again, like he couldn't stop seeing Rob's smug face in his head. "The pleasure was all mine."

He held his gaze on me, and it started to feel like there was something woven into the words he wasn't saying. I wanted so badly to flirt, but I wasn't sure where we were with that, so I simply said, "I had fun getting to know you."

"If you need anything, I'm right next door. Or maybe we can hang out again sometime?" He leaned in closer to me. Slightly. Or maybe I just imagined that part? Okay, I was hopeful, but I was definitely sure he was flirting when he threw in his last comment. "Perhaps walk over instead of driving, though."

It was my turn to throw my head back and laugh. Then I smiled at him, hoping to express my heartfelt appreciation when I said, "Deal."

Ten

Jade

My car drove beautifully, but I still underestimated the time it took to get across town. My manager, Portia, had already switched the closed sign to open when I arrived late. Not that it mattered. Portia was the manager who was everyone's best friend more than a manager. She worked the early shift every day until she could build her matchmaking business. She was amazing at setting people up, and spent more time asking customers about their love interests than making coffee. Her eyes scanned my outfit before she pushed the door open. "Cute Antlers. You're really into this holiday stuff, huh?"

She reminded me to adjust them, and as I straightened them, I replied. "I'm into tips. They are almost double when I dress up. This is the latest costume I found at Goodwill last week. I'm not sure yet, but I think it will be even better than the elf."

I followed her back behind the counter, and we both grabbed aprons and put them on. "Are you still struggling?" Her brows dipped, but she kept her gaze low as if she was allowing me some privacy. "I thought the new apartment was supposed to solve all your money issues."

"It will," I assured her. "But it will take a few months until I get ahead, and now this weekend, I'd like to send gifts home to my parents, but I'm afraid it's already too late."

I didn't think it was possible, but her brows fell even more. "Oh, I forgot that you don't have family here. It's a bummer you can't visit for the holidays." Her head jolted back, and her eyes opened wider. "You should let me set you up for a Christmas—"

"No, no, no." I wagged my finger at her, then turned my back and went down the line, switching on the espresso machines. "I'm completely okay with being single." I turned the coffee grinder on, and refilled it with beans, fully done with that conversation, but Portia pressed on.

"I know you needed some time after your last breakup, but it might be good to get out there again. I just recruited another cute guy from the hardware store. He would be *perfect* for you. When's the last time you went on a date?"

I stared forward, recalling the weekend. I wasn't sure if I could credit myself for going on a date. It was a fake date, but in an odd way it had felt real. I had woken up this morning, thinking about how sweet Evan was for fixing my car, and I still giggled every time I thought about the cheesecake, and Greta trapping me. Portia was probably right about it being way too long to wait after a breakup, but right now, I wasn't interested in dating. But the fake dating was fun. Fewer expectations. "I don't know, Portia. I'm not the single-and-ready-to-mingle type." To bring my point home, I reached into a bag of chips I had stashed below the counter for snacking, retrieved one, and popped it into my mouth. Speaking through a mouthful, I said, "I'm more in the single-and-ready-to-Pringle stage."

She snickered, then opened the fridge to open milk cartoons. "Some people walk around with rose colored glasses; you are the opposite. You walk around with gray ones."

It was my turn to snicker, because she had a point. "Yeah, gray, clouded, scratched, and sat on."

She moved to the dessert case, filling it with fresh muffins, which reminded me of Pearl's cake. "Say," I began. "Are you open to sampling some delicious cheesecake as prospect to sell?"

Her eyes became "are-you-kidding-me" narrow. "Is cheesecake ever a question?"

"Right?" I grinned, excitement budding in my chest. I desperately wanted to make amends with Pearl. "I thought I'd ask before I sprang it on you."

"You can spring cheesecake on me any time, but remember that new owner, Christian, took over yesterday and he now has the final say, and well, we both know he's . . ."

"Blah."

"I meant to say a grump, but blah works, too." Her gaze skirted to the counter, and she swapped her sympathetic expression for a "may-I-help-you" grin. "What can I get you today?" she asked the customer.

"I'm actually here to see Jade, if that's okay."

I hadn't even heard anyone come through the squeaky front door, but my ears perked, immediately recognizing Evan's voice. I spun on my heel, finding him standing just on the other side of counter. He was back to wearing jeans and one of those relatable millennial-hoodies that made him look snuggly. Though he was smiling, there was strain in his eyes. "Hi," I greeted him, suddenly questioning my decision to wear antlers. At least my embarrassed flush wouldn't be apparent under the red-painted cheeks and nose. "You're up early today."

"I wanted to catch you before you got into your morning rush." He held up a pair of black boots, the tags still on, and placed them on the counter. "And I got you these."

My eyes cemented on the shoes. They were obviously genuine leather and expensive with the size 6 ½ sticker still attached. As sweet as that was, my intuition told me they came at a price. I took a step closer to the counter and lowered my voice. "What's up?"

Rubbing the side of his face, he also took a step forward. "My cousin Rob texted me. I think he suspects we aren't really dating. He had all these questions for me. Not that it's any of his business." A disgruntled expression took over his face.

"So not his business," I filled in the pause with conviction.

"Right?" He gestured toward me. "I was worried he might come in and ask you the same questions, to see if we had the same answers. I mean, he asked me what we liked to do for dates, and I made the mistake of telling him that you love movies, and then the next thing I knew, he asked if we'd want to double tonight."

I let out a graceful snort as the thought of going to a movie with Evan's ex-fiancée was absurd, but his lips didn't even bend. "Wait a second. You told them we would, didn't you?"

His lips curled into a cringy smile "I'll buy you another fender.".

I let out a forced laugh as the thought of getting into another car accident was overwhelming. "Hopefully, I don't need another one for a long time." Evan didn't have to offer me anything. I enjoyed spending time with him, and I had nothing to do tonight. "I'll go."

Now, his lips curled into a real smile, one that I definitely loved. It held relief, as well as mischief . . . and maybe a hint of flirtation. Or maybe I was hoping for flirtation?

"Do you think we can rehearse a little this time? I didn't realize how hard it was going to be.

I matched his mischievous smile. "I get off at three."

A string of chatty female customers entered the front door, lining up behind Evan. He checked behind his shoulder, and then stepped to the side, clearing the way. "The movie's at seven, but I'll come over early."

"Sounds good." I motioned to the espresso machine. "Did you want a coffee?"

"Nah. I'm good. I was only here to see you."

I blinked, feeling that in my soul. I understood he was here for this whole business transaction, but somewhere inside me, it felt fantastic to be wanted. It had been forever since I had a guy visit me at work. Why couldn't this be real? I resisted the urge to slam my head into the wall mournfully. Instead, I held up my hand and wiggled my fingers in a feminine wave. "Okay. I'll see you later." I went right into taking customer orders. I worked my entire shift, but I couldn't tell you one thing a customer had said. I was so distracted, thinking about my fake date.

I wasn't ready to date.

So not ready.

But fake dating was exciting.

When my shift was over, I counted my tips, and it was the most I'd ever made. "Two hundred and thirteen dollars and seventy-five cents," I called out as I split the equal piles between Portia and me.

"I guess Rudolph is the way to go," Portia said.

"I guess." I stowed my neatly organized stack of bills into my wallet and held onto the change as I made my way outside and scouted for the bell-ringing Santa. He was always there, and I knew I couldn't walk away without at least dropping something into his bucket. Today, Santa was short, with big chocolate eyes, and braces on his teeth. He also was going for the clean-shaven look as he only had a Santa hat and no beard. I smiled at him and pushed my quarters into the slot one by one.

"What is your Christmas wish?" Santa asked, while sliding a candy cane out of his bag, presenting it to me.

My brow quirked. Did they get paid to ask that because that was the exact same thing the dread-lock Santa had asked? "Um, well," I mused as things were looking up since I was last asked that question. I had a stack of tips, a fixed car, and even a fake date. I wasn't going to push it by getting too excited and I kept my same wish. "I wish that bad stuff stops happening to me so I can get ahead of the bad stuff that has already happened."

"Merry Christmas," he said with a definitive tone and pushed the candy cane closer to me.

"Thank you." I received the gift and called back, "Merry Christmas to you, too!" My phone started to vibrate in my pocket, and I pulled it out to answer, noting the caller ID. "Hey. Mom."

"How are you doing?"

"Not bad. Just leaving work." I pulled my keys from my purse, jingling as I strode to my car with a little pep in my step. "What about you?"

"Same old, but I was calling to tell you that the middle school had an opening to teach eighth grade history. I mentioned to Principal Ron that you had a history degree you aren't using, in addition to teaching experience. He said he'd love to see your application."

"Mom." I started, then stopped, giving myself time to think. "That's very thoughtful of you to think of me, and you're right. I do have a history degree, but I live here."

"Right," she quipped, "But you're working at a coffee shop."

Flashing my eyes heavenward, I inhaled a deep breath. I reached my car, unlocked my door, and got inside, remaining quiet the entire time. Once I started my car, I finally said, "I know it wasn't your plan for me, but I like working at a coffee shop. The amount of stress I had teaching wasn't good for me. I learned I wasn't meant to teach tiny, or even mid-sized humans."

"Well, it doesn't hurt to put in an application," she pressed. "Have you applied to any other teaching jobs?"

I could have restated that I had a job, or explained to her again that my teaching license wasn't valid without the fellowship program, but she obviously wasn't hearing that part. She never heard that part. "Mom, I gotta go," I rushed out. "I'm about to pull into traffic and want to pay attention. Love you, bye." I didn't feel bad when I ended the call, because I had learned my mom and I had different visions for my life. I wasn't going to change her mind, and it would only hurt our relationship if I tried. I loved my mom, and for the sake of our relationship, I avoided certain topics altogether. I was about to put my phone down, but it quickly lit up with a text.

Evan: I may have run into Rob again. I might need to go over some notes with you. Can I come over early?

I didn't even try to hold back my chuckle. The poor guy was in over his head. It's a good thing his cousin lived out of state, and he'd be leaving soon.

Me: I'll be ready.

I set my phone down in the center console, letting my eyes linger on Evan's text. For the first time in a long time, I had plans to go out. Sure, it wasn't a real date, but that didn't mean I couldn't enjoy the movie and have a good time. Evan was handsome but he didn't act like it, which made him even more attractive. Plus, he made me laugh. Not just a little laugh. I can't ever remember a time recently I laughed until I cried. Extra plus, he was super sweet, fixing my car. That made me heart him so much.

My gaze drifted to the side.

If I didn't know better from how my nerves fluttered in my stomach, I'd think I was going on an actual date. I shook my head and put my car in gear, pulling out of my parking space. I didn't need to have these thoughts.

But then again, he was single.

And I was single.

Maybe I was ready to mingle?

Eleven

Evan

Chainsaws are just big butter knives, right? I checked over my shoulder as if I had expected someone to answer that. Then I stared at the tool I had borrowed from my parents' garage. It wasn't one of those loud, gas-powered ones. This was compact and battery operated.

Sensible.

It's no secret I leaned more toward tree hugger—with my zip hoodies and Hey Dudes—than lumberjack, but Discovery Channel was my jam. I watched every season of American Loggers, and I had the major points noted.

Chainsaw.

Red flannel shirt.

And lack-of-shaving-effort facial hair.

Safety goggles. I chuckled, as I positioned my goggles over my eyes, remembering Jade in hers the other night. She was adorable.

Inhaling deeply, I filled my lungs and straightened my spine.

I was ready, but there was a slight catch.

I HATED heights.

Not a little bit bothered by them, but full-blown anxiety attacks.

I was going to push through it because I'm doing this for Jade. She's going out with me again tonight, and it's only fair I repay her in some way. Because she wouldn't do this unless she had a reason to.

Would she?

Tilting my head, I lingered on that thought. I enjoyed spending time with her. Better than enjoyed, I was looking forward to seeing her again. Everything from her mischievous, fun smile, to how her presence had this warming effect on me.

A car alarm blared from somewhere in the neighborhood, and pulled me from my thoughts, reminding me I had a job to do. Without another moment of contemplation, I stuck my foot on the lowest branch. I slowly lifted myself as I tested its strength under my weight.

It held. I let out a sigh of relief and gave the tree a friendly thank-you pat.

It was a girthy branch. It didn't creak as I brought my second foot up and balanced my weight. Lucky for me, I knew the branches of this tree by heart. Not because I climbed them. Remember, the heights thing. Nope, I used to hide behind this tree daily in my youth when we played hide and seek. Back in the days before the internet, where you would get lost outside every day, until your mom screamed at you from the porch with her curlers in. The lamp posts were our alarms, and our bikes were our preferred method of transportation.

A lot has changed since then.

I hoisted the saw over my shoulder and gripped the branch above with my free hand. That branch was like a titanium beam; it was so sturdy. I pulled myself up with ease. I was getting the hang of this working by the sweat of my brow thing. I cocked my head to the side, stretching my neck out. It felt good to be active in the fresh air.

Manly.

And so easy.

All I had to do was shimmy over and saw off the low-hanging branch, and I'd be golden with plenty of time to get ready for my date with Jade. It felt good to say that, too. "I have a date with Jade," I said aloud casually, and I scooted one foot in front of the other. "Because I do that now. I date again."

Snap!

I jerked my foot back, as I apparently had gone too far. I was in between two branches now. Standing on one, but I also had another thick branch at my shoulder level I used as a guardrail.

Safety first.

I breathed, knowing this was only going to take a moment. "Just a quick snip," I hummed out loud as I steadied my weight on both legs and focused on maintaining balance as I found the power switch.

The saw powered on with no problem, and I eyed the narrowest part of the branch for the perfect place to slice. I needed to get a little lower. I crouched, feeling the stretch in my hamstrings, but it was a good stretch. I lowered my saw to the branch, bracing for impact. It was slick and made a nice clean cut; nothing jerky, or dangerous, at all. I cut halfway through the branch as they do on AxMan, and then gravity took over, and I could feel it giving out on its own. I retracted my saw and held onto the branch over me as I watched it break.

It fell brilliantly to the ground, not hitting a thing. Clearly, I was such a natural. I could give a YouTube tutorial on this. Or maybe even a weekend side gig? I'm sure there are plenty of elderly ladies who need a big strong man to take down their low-hanging branches. I straightened the collar on my flannel shirt, thoroughly impressed with myself. Leaning over, I inspected what a clean cut I had made.

Maybe I could have been a surgeon?

Who knew I had this talent?

I couldn't wait to tell Jade she could sleep now, and I quickly—too quickly, maybe a little carelessly—stood up, and smacked my face right into my rail branch. I wasn't positive, but mostly sure my tooth cracked. It was evident when I saw something white fly out of my mouth. Pushing my tongue forward into the massive gap in my teeth that wasn't supposed to be there.

Yep, now I needed a dentist.

But it was after office hours, and I had a date. Pushing my tongue back into the gap, I tried to measure the size of the hole. I wonder if she would even notice?

Who was I kidding? It was right in the middle of my face!

Of course, she would notice. It's not like I had time to grow a mustache. My eyes swelled as the lumberjack facial hair suddenly made so much sense. What I wouldn't give for a big burly mustache to hide behind right now.

Rubbing the barely-there stubble on my chin, I had a thought. I didn't have time to grow one but there were other options. A smirk grew on my lips as I lowered myself onto the next branch. I had an idea. A brilliant idea, and just enough time to execute it.

Twelve

Jade

I was feeling good about tonight. Dressed in jeans and a fitted knit shirt, I was comfortable. I wasn't overdoing it by trying too hard. However, I won't pretend I'm not excited for tonight. I thought about Evan and how he looked at me when I fell on him in the kitchen. I couldn't deny there'd been sparks.

If the chance arose, I was going to tell him I started to have feelings for him.

The doorbell rang and I pushed through the nerves, pinned a smile on my face and opened the door. My gaze skirted to the side, landing on Evan oddly leaning on the door frame with one arm like he was having a hard time standing. "Good evening," his voice rolled out as if he was out of breath.

He was wearing an ugly red Christmas sweater with pine trees on it, and huge pants with gold suspenders. I blinked, trying not to stare. What happened to his hoodie? I shifted my gaze to his face, and almost jumped back. I didn't want to offend him, but I had no idea what that thing was on his face. Facial hair didn't grow that fast, and this was so puffy it didn't look dead! I fought the urge to swat at it with my purse to make sure it didn't bite.

He had a full beard and mustache a shade too light to match his hair, so it was clearly fake.

Was that supposed to be attractive?

I guess it was a style choice. Not one I would make personally, but I wouldn't judge.

Maybe he was dressing this way for Holly? Maybe this was her jam?

Rob had a mustache, so maybe this was his way of competing? I bit my lip, reminding myself this whole fake dating thing had always been about impressing Rob and Holly, but I couldn't deny that my gut twisted. "Ah, heeey," I finally managed to say. It came out as if it had three syllables, with each syllable higher than the previous octave. I clenched my purse close to my body, all my previous excitement for the date draining. Perplexed, I pushed through it. "I'm ready."

He finally stood up straight, taking his arm off my door frame. "The movie tonight is the Grinch. I got tickets online, but then saw they were having a contest for the couple who dresses up as the best character from the movie. I couldn't let an opportunity to win against Rob go by, and I already knew you love to dress up. However, I didn't have much time, so I went with Bricklebaum. What do you think?"

Letting out a huge sigh of relief, I almost chuckled when I finally understood this was a costume. Actually, now that I didn't have to pretend not to be alarmed, I assessed it, and he looked perfect. "Ah, I couldn't even tell you were wearing a costume for a moment," I admitted truthfully.

"I didn't want you to stress about finding something on short notice, so I got you something, too." He retrieved a bag I hadn't noticed before by his foot, and he pulled out items one by one: a yellow sweater, matching earmuffs, and a pink scarf. He paused after each item as if he were waiting for me to solve the mystery. When the last item was out, he said, "You can say no, but I thought you'd make a great Izzy."

My lips fell slightly agape, as I let it sink in how sweet this was for him to plan my costume. I didn't even know what to say. "Ah, why Izzy?"

His lips pinched together, and it was obvious he was holding back a laugh. It went on forever, and I was convinced he'd never tell me what was up. I was about to twist his arm to squeeze out his joke, he managed, "You already have the goggles to pull this off."

"Of course." I easily made fun of myself. He was right. It was perfect, and a huge smile grew on my face because this sounded so fun. "Give me a second. I'll grab them." I excitedly stepped back from the door, and hurried to my closet, retrieving the goggles, not wasting a moment to pull them over my head. I knew Evan would be smiling when I looked back at him, and his grin did not disappoint. There was no way we could ever be serious about this, and I loved it. I snatched the button up sweater from him and slipped it over my shirt. A rush of laughter fell from my lips as I grabbed the earmuffs and scarf. I had the hardest time keeping a straight face. "Oh wait!" I whipped around and ran to my dresser. "I have pink pants!" Snatching up my pants, I rushed to the bathroom and quickly slipped them on. We were both fighting back giggle fits when I was finally dressed and pulled the door closed behind me to walk to his Jeep.

"So. Tell me." I swallowed, trying to be serious, but it was hard to take him seriously when we were both dressed like this. "What are the things I need to know about *us*?"

"Yes, I thought we could rehearse a few things, and we could come up with the perfect relationship." He opened my car door for me, which I thought was sweet, but I still couldn't look at him without laughing. "When is your birthday?"

"July 3rd." I slid into my seat.

He cringed and immediately rebutted. "I accidentally let it slip that we always go skiing on your birthday weekend. I don't even ski, but he doesn't need to know that part, but how does February work?"

He shut my door before I had a chance to reply, ran around to his side, got in, and picked up the conversation where he had dropped it. "We could plan a Valentine's getaway every year."

"That sounds sweet and very couple*ish* but." My brow arched, as I was stuck on the first thing he said. "What do you mean we always go? Didn't we just start dating?"

He started the car and backed out. "Right. We just started dating because that's the only thing that makes sense as to why my parents recently met you, but I thought it would be cool if maybe we've known each other for years. Like maybe we made an annual ski trip with friends, keeping in touch and I'm the reason you found the apartment across from my house."

"Oh." I stared forward as that sort of made sense. "That could work, but how did we know each other? I grew up in the Midwest, and you were—"

"Coding camp."

My forehead started to tighten, as all of the sudden this started to feel more like a job than a date. I was given an assignment and needed to study. "Color coding?"

"No, computer coding. My friends and I always went to a coding camp in the summer, and you were there. You were the only girl in the class. All the guys had a crush on you, but you always sat by me. I thought it was because I had the best snacks. I brought the double pack of chocolate peanut butter cups in my bag, and I opened them to eat, and I looked around for someone to share them with. In a perfect meet cute, I looked to my left and there you were."

I still struggled to take him seriously because I couldn't stop staring at that bush on his face. It took every ounce of strength I had not to look directly at it when he tried to make eye contact with me. This whole thing was ridiculous, yet adorable. I never in a million years even thought I'd find a man who loved to dress up as much as I did. "Isn't that a commercial?"

"No, I think that was the Oreo commercial where the girl split it. This is way more original." He turned left, entered the freeway, and sped up. "I got a little carried away trying to make it believable."

"I guess." I didn't think I was that gullible before but as I sat next to Evan and soaked this all in, I began to wonder if maybe I had missed some warning signs. At this point, I thought I might be going against my better judgement to agree, but I was already in his Jeep, heading to our date. "Okay . . . You like chocolate peanut butter, which makes sense, but I can't code."

He waved dismissively. "It's fine. Nobody is going to ask you to."

"If I knew how to code, does it make sense that I work at a coffee shop?"

"How about, you forgot everything when the chalkboard fell on your head."

I double-blinked, feeling a light headache coming on with all these details. "Say what?"

"It could be the real reason you quit teaching. The school was dilapidated and falling apart."

I eyed the freeway speeding by, admitting it was tempting to jump out to avoid the hole of doodoo getting deeper and deeper. I honestly couldn't tell if he was serious or not. We had come from giggling like kids over our costumes to needing to plan the Geneva convention. The only explanation I could think of for his odd behavior was this whole Rob thing. He really was stuck on winning. "When does this end?"

"Let me check." He held his phone up to eye level while keeping one eye on the road. I still was unable to not see that stupid thing on his face. It wasn't even proportionate to anything realistic. This had to be a prank.

"Let's see, your birthday . . . got that," he mumbled. "Job, coding camp, peanut butter cup, meet-cute."

"Wait for a second," I blurted out, feeling fear creep into my chest. "You forgot; I told them we met because I crashed into your car! Now, none of this backstory makes sense."

"And he busted me on that," he blurted out, holding up a finger and tacked on, "but I was quick and blurted out that's how we reconnected."

"How many questions did he ask? It sounds like an interrogation?"

"He is a lawyer."

My gaze dropped to my lap, and I played with the hem of my sweater. "Do you think he knows? Maybe, that's why he had all the questions."

"No, he can't know. I was so smooth. I never even flinched."

My eyes hooked his mustache, which was starting to go a little slanted, with one side bending up. Swallowing, I thought about what I was getting into. Everything about the tone of the evening had changed in the last fifteen minutes. Before, Evan was this sweet guy who offered to fix my car, and now, he was wearing a disguise while we made up false identities.

Something in the back of my head niggled at me, as Evan was acting so completely insane right now. "Have you ever thought of taking a less passive aggressive approach to winning with Rob?"

"What do you mean? Like punching him in the face," he spurted out. "Sure. Everyday."

I started giggling, wanting so much to rip that slanted mustache off Evan's face.

Had we taken this too far?

I was about to find out.

Thirteen

Evan

By the time I found a parking spot, I was sweating so profusely that my mustache was sliding down my lip. Do most people add glue? I used the included double-sided sticky tape, but apparently it wasn't enough. The package had no instructions or even a warning label about how hot these things were. I should have worn shorts. Plus, I think I had an abnormally small upper lip pallet thingy because even with it sliding down my lip, I had difficulty breathing through my nose.

Too late, though. I couldn't take it off now, because that would be totally weird. There was the issue of my chipped front tooth. It didn't hurt even though it cracked right through the center. Luckily, I found the part that broke off, and dropped it in a cup of water now marinating at home, per Google recommendation until I get into the dentist.

I smiled at Jade as we got out of my Jeep and beelined to the theater. Tugging at my collar, I regretted wearing this furnace sweater, but I had to have the whole 'fit' or it wouldn't look right. I was loudly mouth breathing as I opened the door for Jade.

"I'm really sorry about this." She strolled through the entrance and peered back, waiting for me. Her eyes were slightly narrow, and laser focused on my upper lip. Perhaps she suspected something was up? I couldn't be certain because she had a pleasant smile on her face. I prayed she wasn't miserable, because at this point, I really wanted to impress her, but I had a sinking feeling something was off about her. I just didn't know what.

"It's okay. I was looking forward to a night out." She smiled at me slyly and stood close to me. Not just a little close.

Date close.

My eyes scoured the room, searching for Rob and Holly. Maybe Jade was being extra prepared, but I saw no sign of them. Taking a cue from her, I grabbed her hand. She didn't flinch as she received my hand in hers.

We had the perfect arm lengths for holding hands.

"They leave town tomorrow, so this will be the last time for sure we have to do this, and I hope I can make it up to you."

Before she could reply, Rob's boisterous voice sliced through the air. "Hey, cousin." I turned toward them, careful to give them my new Bricklebaum gaze, but they both stopped dead in their tracks.

Rob was dressed as the Grinch, which frankly didn't surprise me, but Holly didn't have a costume. I'd assumed she would dress as Cindy-Lou Who, with her long blonde hair, but she would have to at least braid her hair to resemble Cindy. She wasn't even wearing pink or anything remotely passable as Christmas. She had on a long black sweater dress, and heels, and her hair was pulled back in a messy bun. I tried not to stare, but she must have sensed my confusion because she pulled up one side of her lips into an awkward smile the way she always did when she was insecure. "I didn't know I needed to dress up."

"Oh, no." My jaw fell, as I recalled I had texted Rob about the contest, assuming he would tell Holly. "I didn't think I needed to tell you because I told Rob."

Her eyes slid to Rob, who didn't even defend his choice to not get her a costume. He raised his chin and guessed at our costumes. "Mr. Bricklebaum and Izzy."

I didn't want to draw attention to my tooth, so I ran a hand over my beard smoothing it and casually said, "Glad you could tell."

"It's not hard." Rob's laugh rushed out. "My first guess would be a woolly caterpill—" Holly elbowed him hard, cutting off his words, and his face instantly flushed red. Holly didn't bend a lip at him as she crossed her arms and stood a good foot away from him. They resembled sworn enemies standing like that, rather than two people who were supposedly newly engaged. "Oh, before I forget." Rob reached into a small shopping bag he had hooked on his arm, and pulled out a set of stuffed antlers, presenting them to Jade. "I saw this when I grabbed my costume. I had assumed you'd dress up as the dog. I had pegged you for an animal lover and thought it would be funny if I gave you the antlers like the Grinch does in the movie."

"Ah." Jade let out a low nervous chuckle. "Nope, not a dog. Sorry." She turned her shoulder away from Rob, leaning closer to me.

I was completely disgusted, though not surprised, Rob forgot Holly's costume while trying to suck up to Jade. That's just the tool he was. Feeling completely offended for Jade, that Rob would even think of getting her a gift, I leaned closer as well, asking, "Are you ready to go into the theater?" I wavered a little at the end because I wasn't sure if I should add a nickname or other term of endearment. I decided to leave it open. I wasn't the best at fake dating, but Jade on the other hand, was a fantastic actress.

She stepped closer to me, erasing the small gap between us. I could smell the swirls of her warm vanilla scent again. Man, she smelled amazing. When she latched her lashes back up on me, she had her competitive expression. Wrapping her free arm around my waist, she said, "I'm ready to snuggle you."

Her touch was smoldering. The mere friction of her hand wrapped around my waist sent a spark right through my body, and I instantly started sweating even more.

It wasn't as bad as that time I accidentally sat on my welding torch, but close.

If Rob wasn't buying this act, then it couldn't be helped, because even I had a hard time discerning what was going on. The heated way Jade studied me made me forget we were faking this.

Give this girl an Emmy.

I guided her forward, not glancing back at Rob or Holly because I had an impossible time breaking my gaze from Jade. We must have looked like a pair of love birds who couldn't get close enough. As soon as I sat down, she scooted so close to me, I easily slipped my arm around her. Her look-of-love performance put me at ease. I had almost forgotten we weren't even on a date. Everything about her was so perfect. From how her petite little body fit perfectly in my arm, to the way the top of her head brushed against the bottom of my chin. Man, did I mention she smelled amazing?

The only bad thing was the mustache was a little more animated than the instructions had mentioned. It had a life of its own. A life filled with dancing all over my face. Maybe it's because I was sweating so much from this sauna sweater, but every few minutes the 'stache would creep down to my top lip. I was smooth though, and I placed my hand on my chin, tilting my head away from Jade as if deep in thought. As soon as my head was at the perfect angle of an isosceles triangle. I would casually rub my chin, and discreetly push my mustache back into place.

It was an art.

And I was Picasso.

The perfect fidget device.

I was preoccupied with keeping my 'stache on my face, and fielding those dreamy looks Jade kept flashing at me, I never even once looked over at Rob or Holly. I had forgotten they were even there.

We were halfway through the movie, and I had completed another successful angle-tuck-and-slide 'stache sequence as I turned my face to snuggle her. The top of her head was like the warmest little nest made just for me. I nestled into it, and then it happened . . .

The corner of my 'stache got stuck to her hair!

I gave my head a backward tug, but her hair pulled tight and she jolted slightly.

Not good!

Nightmare!

I scooted closer, giving her hair some slack. I was so close to her now there wasn't even a slice of air between us as I hovered my face over the center of her head, assessing the situation. It didn't seem to bother her, though. She only cuddled tighter to me.

I didn't mind that part. Though the face trap was a tad disturbing.

Yep, I had trapped a lock of hair like a mouse's tail right to my face.

I flexed my lip up and down, side to side. I couldn't get her hair to fall out.

I poked my index finger underneath the edge of my mustache, trying to brush the hair out. It was hopelessly stuck to my face. Two seconds ago, it was sliding off my face but now it wouldn't budge.

I had to do something.

I was in a hairy situation.

Someone was going to notice soon.

I could pull her hair and pray she didn't notice or I could rip my 'stache off.

Ripping my mustache off would hurt. I eyed the top of her head. Maybe she wouldn't feel anything if I ripped it out fast enough? I wrapped my fingers around the edge of the 'stache, ready to pull. It was the only way to free us. I held my breath, counting to three. One. Two. Three. Then like a perfectly executed dance sequence—okay, not even close—I yanked. She yelped, jumping to her feet right in the center of the theater.

The mustache stuck to her hair and boomeranged back at her like a giant wooly caterpillar in flight. Waving her hands in the air, she sucked in a squealing breath, and I plugged my ears, waiting for it . . .

"Ouch!" She yelped from the tug on her hair. All the eyes in the theatre were on her. She had gargantuan air sacs for lungs that belted on forever like an opera singer singing her last note. In a moment so fast, I didn't have time to think, I wrapped one arm around her waist, swooping her into me and planted my lips right on hers, silencing her scream.

She was the most brilliant impromptu actress, not missing a beat, kissing me back as if my lips were the only thing that could save her life.

Taking my chance, I slid my hand up to her hair, snatching the 'stache back before breaking the kiss. Breathless, my eyes dropped to hers. It didn't take me more than a second to know she hadn't faked that kiss. The inflections in her eyes were honest and dialed into me. If we weren't standing in the back of a movie theater, I would have . . . I'd . . . I don't know what I would do because this wasn't part of the plan.

I inhaled measured breaths as I stared back at her. I didn't have the words to explain what had happened. I held up the mustache and shrugged.

Someone behind us yelled at me to sit down. I wanted to sit down, but my face was like a used circus stage. Half sticky, and slimy from the glue mixed with sweat. The other half burned from where it was ripped off. I'm sure my lip was swollen from the tree branch, in addition to the chipped tooth. I was feeling overly exposed. I held the stache again and leaned forward, whispering in her ear, "I'll explain after the movie, but I need to go wash my face. I'll be right back."

Nodding softly, her eyes never left me. As I walked away, I did some math. The looks she had been giving me all night, plus the way she kissed. . . I had a hard time thinking she could really be that good an actress.

I entered the empty bathroom, and crossed over to the sink, squinting through the pinching as I ripped off the beard and splashed cooling water on my face. I used a paper towel to wipe it off. I was a mess. My hair was drenched from sweat, shining like I had gelled it. The stupid sweater was an abysmal failure. I had no idea what I was thinking, but now that the mustache was gone, the sweater had to go, too. I slipped it off and threw it in the trash.

There I was.

Me again.

Except for the fat lip and tooth stub, but really it wasn't that bad.

Now to explain to Jade what had gotten into me.

That meant I had to confess to cutting down her tree, but I was oddly excited to tell her that. Then it struck me. I had completely removed every ounce of Holly from my heart.

She didn't have a hold on me the way she had before.

Something had happened.

I didn't even have to think twice about what that thing was.

All I thought about as I stood here was getting back to Jade.

And it felt amazing.

Basketball tossing the paper towel into the trash, I flinched when it landed six inches away. Nobody saw it. It didn't count. I rebounded it, dunking as I hurried out of the door.

It was much better with the costume off. I could breathe again. Rushing around the corner, I didn't even notice when I almost walked right into Holly.

"Oh, hey," she blurted as if she was trying to get my attention.

I checked behind her, looking for Rob, but she was alone. I motioned down the hall in the direction I was going. "Hey, I'm headed back—"

She pushed her hand forward, touching my arm. I was frozen. "Can you wait a sec?"

"What is going on?" I asked, but then my eyes sprang open wide when I noticed the tip of her nose was red, as it looked like she had been crying. She must be upset with Rob. I mean, who wouldn't get annoyed by him? She chose him though. It's not like their relationship was any of my business. I placed my hand on hers, mostly to remove her hand from mine. I tried to think of the perfect something to say that told her I didn't want to be dragged into her Rob's drama. It's not that I was heartless, but I was not the right person. Maybe I could send Jade to talk to her about this stuff, or better yet, she could talk to him. "Holly, I think this is something you need to talk to Rob about—"

"Rob just stole Jade," she blurted out, sealing her eyes on mine in a way that told me she was a thousand percent serious. "They just left together."

"What?" I scoffed at her weird diversion, totally ready to blow off this ridiculous assumption, but Holly went on rambling, "Rob does this thing where he pursues a woman so subtly, but with so much vigor. He did it to me, and I've been watching the signs this whole time, and he just did it to Jade. It's a game to him to steal your girlfriends. When he did it to me, I got confused, and as soon as he had me, it was like I was his trophy. All he wanted to do was put me on a shelf and brag to everyone that he stole me from you. I realized it wasn't about me, it was this weird thing about you. He's awful. I've been wanting to tell you for so long. Rob would check my phone, but I came back to find you to warn you, so you can stop Jade before she ruins her life too."

"Ah . . ." My gaze quickly fell away from hers as I tried to think of what to say. It was the oddest thing I had ever experienced. Was she saying this to get me to distrust Jade? But then my mind planted on the weird gift Rob gave Jade, and all the weird extra attention he gave Jade at my house.

Could Holly be right? No way. This had to be some skit for me to doubt Jade. "I need to find Jade," I said, my gaze skirting to the side at the rush of people exiting the theater. The movie was over. It would only be a moment, and Jade and Rob would be looking for us. "Come on." I nodded to the crowd. "Let's not leave them waiting."

But they weren't waiting.

They weren't anywhere.

After waiting for the slew of people to pass in front of us until the last person was out of the theater, Rob and Jade never came. I took a frantic lap around the theater, thinking maybe they were somewhere, but they were gone. "They left without us."

I looked at Holly, who swallowed, nodding through it like it would help her to breathe. She looked broken. I could only imagine how horrible her life was with Rob. He clearly tricked her, but she had a chance to start over.

"Something bad had to have happened," I added as I checked my phone, already en route to my Jeep. There was no way Jade would ever leave with Rob.

Unless Holly was right.

Did Rob steal Jade?

He had done this before.

That was not going to happen again! I steeled my chin, scanning the parking lot until I spotted my Jeep but not Rob's rental car. I dialed Jade's number, pressing my ear to the phone, and called after Holly, "I'll give you a ride to my grandma's if you want. It's on my way, but we must hurry. I will not let Rob get to her."

Fourteen

Evan

I pulled into my grandma's narrow driveway and didn't put my Jeep in park before announcing, "Here you go."

Holly stared forward. Her fair-skinned cheek twitched as if she was feigning deep in thought. I didn't want to waste time because I had to get to Jade, but I couldn't push Holly out the car door. Maybe I could offer to walk her to the door? That might get her out of here faster.

Too late.

Rob manifested on the front porch, strutting towards us with his shoulders back, obviously displaying his lofty sense of superiority. Just one time, I wanted to punch him in the face. My nostrils flared, unbidden. If I found out he did anything or said anything to Jade, I wasn't going to be able to hold it back.

Holly finally moved, getting out of my Jeep, and I already put the Jeep in reverse when she ran past Rob, not even acknowledging him. That jerk didn't even try to talk to her either, he just kept pacing toward my Jeep.

On any other day, I could have let it roll off my back. Not today.

I shifted the Jeep into park, and rolled my window down, calling out, "What did you say to Jade?"

"Maybe if you'd pay more attention to your woman, you'd know." His head bobbled, as if it was too fat to stay balanced on his scrawny shoulders.

I wrung my hands together, fighting back every urge I had to not strangle him. It didn't make sense Jade would ask him for a ride home. He had to be lying about something. The problem with trying to talk to a liar, though, is they aren't going to tell you the truth. My attempt to give him a chance to be honest was clearly futile.

I was done wasting time with this cantankerous jerk. I needed to find Jade. I had a mission. A mission Rob insisted on interrupting when he blubbered out the stupidest thing, "Looks like you lost another girl, huh?"

"What's that, Robby?" I didn't think twice before I jumped out of my Jeep, pulling my shoulders back. "You need help shutting your mouth?"

I grabbed his shirt collar, roughing him closer to me and jerked my fist back, ready to flatten his smirk. My heart swelled, as this was going to be better than a decade of therapy. The front door opened, Grandma hollered out, "Oh, heavens, Evan, no!"

My fists shook, but I didn't want to give my granny a heart attack. I flattened my palm and raked it through my hair, the tension seething in my fingers. "You're so lucky you got saved by a ninety-year-old lady," I whispered under my breath, as I ground my molars.

"Rob," Granny called out, her voice taking an inquiring tone. "Something's wrong with Holly. She's in here packing and crying. She said you're a loser, and a jerk. You'd better come talk to—"

"Coming!" He cut her off, sprinting forward as if he was a scared cat with his tail between his legs. I could hear Holly screaming in the background and it was getting louder. Before Rob could duck inside the house, Holly was on the porch, not slowing her steps. Her brows beaded together, her entire expression is thunderous. "I was just coming inside to check on you," Rob squawked out.

"Don't bother." Her boots clicked across the wood planks on the porch until she stopped in front of Rob. "I'll tell you exactly how I feel about you right now." Raising her hand, as if she's ready to spike a volleyball, she swiped at the air until her palm loudly cracked against his cheek.

I couldn't help but sputter out a laugh. It was all coming full circle, and I didn't even have to break my fist to make it happen. Talk about a Christmas miracle. Now, I needed to get to Jade.

Fifteen

Jade

I kept my phone silent and all the lights in my apartment dark as I hid below the window and peeked. Evan stood in his window, staring this way with his phone attached to his ear. My phone had been blowing up continuously, since I had left the theater with Rob. I just needed to get away. I had lost myself in the date. Somewhere between arriving and settling in, I had forgotten we were faking it, and I one hundred thousand percent felt we were on a real date.

It was the start of something.

While I waited for him to get back from the bathroom, I went to refill my drink, and Rob came out. He told me the reason he didn't get Holly a costume was because he had found messages from Evan on Holly's phone. They were planning on getting back together. Rob was upset, but still came to the movie to see if they'd confess. When they didn't, he was so disgusted, he had to tell me the truth.

Faceplanting into the palm of my hands, I cringed. How could I be so stupid? This whole thing was a sham to make Evan's ex-fiancée jealous. I knew THAT from the beginning. Of course, he was fine using me to make Holly jealous.

My ears literally burned from embarrassment as I thought about how I had kissed Evan.

When Rob dropped me off, he felt so bad for me that I was sucked into this drama, he offered his Grinch costume, since he knew I loved dressing up. It felt odd, but I took it, knowing I had to work in the morning. Maybe a part of me wanted it to spite Evan.

Now, I crawled on the floor to my bed, careful not to cross in front of my window. I should have known better than to get involved with the man next door. Now I was a prisoner in my own home. I slipped into the bed, pulling the covers tight and shut my eyes and waited for the rhythmic-not-lullaby-branch thumping to cement my headache.

But it never came.

I yanked the blanket back, and sat up, listening. The wind howled as if it was getting ready for a kite festival, but no thumping.

What happened to my branch?

I got up, beelined to the window, and did the fastest peak and sneak I could, confirming the branch was *gone.*

There was only one person that would have chopped down that branch.

Somewhere inside me, my soul screamed. Life wasn't fair. I'd finally found the most amazing and conscientious man, and he was in love with the mean girl who didn't deserve him.

I flung back down on my bed, flopping a pillow over my head. Now it wasn't the sound that kept me awake but the absence of it. Not because I had gotten used to it, but because it reminded me of Evan.

Sixteen

Jade

I was late to work the next day, but it had nothing to do with a lost shoe, a crashed car or even a branch that kept me up all night. For the first time in a while, everything was fixed. At least the logistical stuff was, but I couldn't say the same about my heart.

Dressed in the Grinch costume Rob had given me, I truly felt drained of all Christmas spirit, and I dragged my feet. My heart was clouded, and I didn't even rush the last steps into the coffee house. Santa was set up in his usual spot, and I somberly waved. "Hey, Santa."

"What's your Christmas wish?" His smile was jolly underneath his classic Santa white beard.

I paused, wondering why these fake Santa's felt they could ask me personal questions all the time. It's not like we're friends. "What's with the invasive question?"

"Socratic Method."

"Socrat—what?" I quirked a brow at him.

"Socrates believed everyone with a problem already knew the answer, as long as you asked them the right question."

I parked one hand on my hip, and barked out, "Who said I had a problem?"

"People are scared to ask the question because they are afraid of the answer." He winked at me, sending a shiver down my spine like something I had never felt. "It's okay. I already know your wish." He nodded to the shop. "He's here."

"Who's here?" I asked haughtily, stretching my neck like a crane trying to see through the tinted glass windows. "If who I thought he was talking about was in there, then clearly Santa was senile.

Evan was not my Christmas wish.

I stomped forward, zipping through the door, hoping Portia wouldn't notice I was late, but then I dug my heel into the floor halting fast. Portia wasn't behind the counter. *Christian was here!* He instantly squared his body with mine, checked his wristwatch and flashed it at me.

"Sorry, I'm late." I beelined back to the pantry and grabbed an apron, tying it on, while speed walking to clock in. "Where's Portia?"

He walked in front of the computer, partially blocking it from me. "I switched shifts with her." His eyes were narrowed, and he held his lips tight.

"Oh." I deadpanned, not having time to examine my thoughts before Christian continued.

"I cross checked your schedule with your time ins, and I don't think you have ever been on time."

Cringing, I forced a breezy tone. "I had a rough week. I moved across town and still struggling to find the fastest way—" My voice dropped off, because he stuck his hand in front of the computer screen, blocking it.

"Don't bother clocking in." His voice was even. Stern.

"What?" I whispered.

"I'm sorry," he firmly continued. "We need to cut payroll."

"I'm great with customers," I squeaked out, placing a hand on my chest. "I dressed up as the Grinch."

He paced to the counter, removed an envelope and handed it to me. "I'm sorry, but we've been too slow."

"Christmas is tomorrow." My words were more matter-of-fact than sad. I was so totally stunned, my feet glued to the floor. How would I be getting fired again?

He motioned to the envelope. It wasn't lost on me that his Rolex glinted in the light. Being an owner of a chain of coffee shops, he never spared himself luxury. It wasn't fair. My measly wage was nothing to him. He didn't care. "That's your last week's pay, and a small severance pay."

Blinking back tears, I slid one foot away, as I didn't want him to see me like that. "You said I was free to go, right?"

His lips thinning into a straight line, but I didn't believe for a moment that he had real empathy for me. "I'm sorry, but I'll be a good reference for you."

"Don't bother," I spit out and spun on my heel practically running, adrenaline pumping through my legs right back out the door I had just entered. There was fat ol' Santa sitting smugly on this stool. "Hey you!" I called, not caring that I was picking a fight. "You lied! You said my wish was inside." I flashed my envelope at him and spat out, "But I got fired."

He smiled at me, lifting his chin the slightest bit in motion. "Look behind you."

I threw my hands up and spun on my heel. "Are you nuts—" My voice dropped off because there was Evan. The last person I wanted to see right now. "Santa. You're killing me," I called over my shoulder, but as I turned, the sidewalk was empty. My eyes about bugged out of my head and I called out, "Santa!?"

"Who are you talking to?" Evan asked in a weary tone.

"Santa was right here two seconds ago." I motioned to the perfect open space.

Evan's lips curled at the corners as if he was sharing a secret. "Jade—"

"Don't tell me I'm crazy because he was right here."

His shoulders bounced slightly as if he was stifling a chuckle. "I'm not going to tell you that."

"Why are you here? To rub it in my face that you got your girlfriend back. Do you want congratulations?"

One of his brows was raised above the other. "What are you talking about?"

"Rob told me you were getting back with her."

His expression sparked as if he had solved a riddle. "That's why you left and are avoiding me?"

"Well, of course it is. I felt like a fool. Bad things always happen to me. I can't believe I got sucked into your weird game."

"What do you mean bad things always happen to you?" Even though I was nearly screaming at him, his voice got even softer, carrying the empathy I'd been dying to have from ANYBODY in my life.

I pressed my palms against my chest—my hands trembled so badly I knew he could see—my heart pounding hard against them. "Have you met me? I just got fired. AGAIN! It's Christmas Eve, and I have no money. Then there's you." I gestured toward him frantically. "I thought I had made a new friend but it became clear to me that you were only using me to get back with your ex—"

"That's not true." He took a step closer and put his hand on my forearm, squeezing it so firmly, I struggled to get away. "I'm not back with her. Stop saying that. I don't ever want to be with her. I want someone else."

"Well, good for you." I didn't even know why I was talking to him. This whole encounter was ridiculous. So embarrassing, and I was over it. I took a few steps off the sidewalk. Evan released his grip on my arm. In a way, it felt as if my heart left go of the pull it had toward him.

He called after me, "Jade, this may suck to hear, but maybe the reason bad things happen to you is because *you're the good thing that has to happen to someone else.*"

Halting my steps, I wanted to scream, "What does that mean?" When I spun back on my heel, I saw moisture in his eyes, and my gut fell. I was silent on the outside, but my heart sent sirens on the inside. His gaze danced around my face, and I waited for him to explain but he didn't. He moved forward, erasing all the space between us. I froze as he slowly lifted his hands to my face, brushing his thumb over my lips.

His eyes entwined with mine as I searched for an explanation. When he finally spoke, his voice squeaked, "I wish we could go back to the beginning, to when I first saw you."

"Why?" I stared forward with my resting Grinch face, waiting for him to blame this whole thing on me.

"Because I was so wrapped up in trying to beat Rob and Holly that I almost missed *you.*"

"I don't understand."

"You were game to engage in my random shenanigans, and along the way I had the most fun I've ever had. I almost missed it, though. I wish we could start over, and I would never ask you to be my fake date. I would ask you to be my real date."

My heart pumped full of all the swoons I had never had. Had Santa been totally right? I let my lips curl into a giant smile while I curled my toes pinching them tight. "What are you waiting for?"

His gaze continued to dance across my face. He looked at me the way I needed to be looked at. Like he was really seeing me. As if his entire world would collapse if I merely suggested I didn't want him. "I wish for that, too," I replied, knowing with all my heart I wanted a chance to get to know Evan for real. To date him for *real*. It was my final Christmas wish.

Epilogue
Jade

I stood behind the Formica counter at the new shop above Evan's mad science lab, tallying the number of cheesecakes I'd sold that week. "Forty-two orders were picked up, and I have another eleven presold for next week."

The smile on Pearl's cherry-painted lips only grew bigger as Evan did the rest of the math. "At fifty dollars a cake, you two made over two thousand with only word-of-mouth advertising the first week."

"That's not bad for a side hustle with no business plan, or even a name." I was proud of what we'd thrown together in the last week. It started as a late Sunday idea that we tossed around. Evan immediately volunteered space in his shop loft for a small commercial kitchen. Everything was modest and done on a budget, but I was amazed how we all pulled together and made it happen.

"Yep, just two chicks bootlegging cake from a computer shop loft," Evan teased, while taking a moment to look at each of us.

"Hey, wait a second," I interjected. "What about Two Chicks Cake Shop?" I wrinkled my nose, letting the name ring in my head. "Is that any good for a name?"

"I like it," Pearl immediately agreed. "I can even visualize someday when we get our own building, we'd have a cute logo with two chickens and barn house decor."

"No, Mom." Evan chuckled, giving his mom his easy grin to let her down gently. "Chicks like women, not birds."

"Oh!" Pearl's eyes rounded. "That makes even more sense. Here, I thought it was something to do with your Discovery animal shows."

We all shared a good laugh, but Evan didn't let the comment die. "I can't even remember the last time I watched one of those shows."

"Really?" His mom's gaze angled in a disbelieving way.

"Yeah," Evan assured her, moving toward the display cases. "Look at everything I've been doing. I work all day. After work, Jade and I remodeled the loft. It's been one thing after another."

"Sorry to keep you so overextended," I teased, with a faux hurt look on my face.

"I didn't mean it like that." Evan slid his arm around me, pulling me into a side hug. "I was saying a lot has changed in the last two months." He leaned his face closer to my ear, and whispered, "But I wouldn't change any of it for the world."

A trickle of goosebumps swirled through me as I felt the same way. I had no idea how I had finally broken my bad luck spree. "Hey, I have an idea," I piped up, as an idea to make Evan happy came into my head. "It's Friday and work is over for the week. Let's celebrate by having one of your famous Discovery Channel marathons. All the alien shows you can cram in."

"Count me out," Evan's mom proclaimed. She dramatically grabbed her coat and slipped it on. She leaned in for a fast hug around Evan's neck. "You two knock yourselves out. I'm ready for bed."

"Love you, Mom," Evan called after her as she was already halfway toward the exit.

"Thanks for a great week," I said, still in disbelief we'd pulled everything off.

"See you both on Monday." She waved goodbye with the jingle of the old-fashioned doorbells signaling she was gone.

Evan turned to me with a gleam in his eye. Not just any gleam. My favorite one. Wrapping one arm around my waist, he pulled me in close to him, and he whispered, "Thank you."

Tilting my head to the side, I gave him a humored expression. "For what? Offering to watch your alien shows with you?"

He rolled his lips inward, drawing attention to them. I had to fight the urge to give them a little smooch, but I waited patiently for him to finish his thought. "For, everything. I don't think I've ever seen my mom so excited about something. You just came into our lives and made it better for everyone. It's like you were the missing piece we didn't even know we needed."

My cheeks blushed as Evan was giving me credit for something I didn't do. They were the ones who did all the heavy lifting. I merely walked beside them and that wasn't a herculean task, because I much enjoyed the view of my handsome boyfriend. "I can't take all the credit." I playfully batted my eyes, adding, "Santa helped."

"Was it Santa?" Evan's eyes narrowed. "Because I seem to recall everything being traced back to that first slice of cheesecake."

"Ah." I threw my head back, and laughed, recalling that day at Evan's mom's. He was right, that was the start of it all. You're right," I agreed. "From now on, the answer to all our life's problems is cheesecake."

Evan nodded, his lips spreading into the most sensational grin, as he leaned down and pressed a kiss to the tip of my nose, and whispered, "Cheesecake is life."

Bonus Epilogue
One year later . . .

"I can't believe it's the last time we clean this place." I dropped my stained rag into the laundry bin in the closet, and soberly turned back to Evan; my arms hung loosely at my sides. "I have no idea where the last year went."

Evan pushed the last tray of cake pans farther into the dishwasher, and shut the door, rocking back on his heels as his gaze regarded mine. There was a slight turn on one side of his lips, but he remained quiet, which frankly drove me nuts. I hadn't seen him all day, as he was working his job. He had arrived to help me clean and perform the emotional lock up. I had spent the day naturally over caffeinated—well, some parts my natural personality and some parts supplemented with caffeine—wanting to chatter about my anxiety. Of course, I recounted all our funniest, scariest, and most random memories about owning this little cakeshop to myself.

It was a little lonely, and so hard to believe it was all coming to an end. Not the way we had dreamed either. We weren't expanding. We weren't moving into a beautiful new building with a coffee bar for me to run. We were shutting up shop. Forever.

Evan's dad retired and to everyone's surprise, including his own, he bought a condo in Florida. It didn't take Pearl more than a moment to trade in her bakery days for a bathing suit and cabana. It turned out Evan never had to move out because his parents moved first. After Thanksgiving, they swiftly crammed thirty years of memories into a U-Haul and gifted the whole house to Evan.

Pearl wasn't available to be my business partner anymore. I didn't feel right using her recipe. That wasn't the total truth either. Turns out, I didn't have the special something to make these cakes. I swore she never gave me the correct recipe because whenever I tried, something was off. I teased it was her special essence, but either way, the cakes were never the same. Frankly, I lost my passion for it once I learned she was leaving.

So, I hit a crossroads with my career again. I swear if I never have to worry about money again in my life, I'd be one happy chicken. Yep, I dressed as a chicken today. We went with the Two Chicks Cheesecake name, and well, the costume was amazing for tips. I fluffed my feathers and went to grab my mop bucket to stow away. As I wheeled it back to the janitorial closet, I savored the glossy tile, and shiny stainless-steel countertops *one more time.*

I had to let it go.

All of it.

I was going to miss this little bakery with its cheesecake charm smells—dark chocolate, and salted caramel, unliked anything you'd find at a market.

Another dream bites the dust.

Unemployed again right before Christmas.

"Something happened today." Evan came up behind me, leaning with one hand on the wall. He stood, framing the hallway, causing my breath to hitch in my chest. *He was still a phenomenal leaner.*

"What's that?" I jimmied the mop bucket into the over-stuffed micro closet and quickly closed it before it rolled back out. It was a slick trick I'd learned earlier this year, and it made me smile to think this was the final time I'd have to do it.

"It started last week when my dad reconnected with an old friend at his retirement party. It turns out, he knew someone who worked for NASA."

"Oh yeah." I slid my over-sized chicken feet forward, until the tips of my toes bumped into the tips of his toes and rapped both hands smugly around his waist. I gazed up at his handsome face, thoroughly inspecting it for the things he wasn't telling me. Yep. He had a squiggle of indistinguishable line right above his brow. I was going to need more details to draw this out of him. "And then what?"

"My dad put in a good word for me, and that guy passed it forward, and I guess I have an internship."

"Say what?" I sputtered out a cough of dust that must have been marinated in my throat since I mopped. "You have a job at NASA?"

"Not just any position. They need a robotics specialist." His lips pitched together, as he cocked his head to the side. It was a flawless expression among many that I loved to stare at. "I accepted."

"Are you kidding me right now? Wait . . . you didn't show them Greta, did you?" I wagged my head back and forth, stalling my reaction as I inspected his expression for signs he was teasing. "Because Greta might not help your case."

"No, I'm totally serious, and I want you to come with me." The spiral of light that rippled through his eyes told me exactly how he was feeling. He leaned forward, tilting his chin down until he was kissing close. I didn't mean to ruin the moment—okay, I'll blame it on my nerves. When he leaned over something caught my eye behind him.

There was a lone cheesecake sitting on the counter that Evan had been standing in front of earlier. We never brought cakes back to the dish area, as they all got stored in the front freezer. Even then, I clearly remembered we sold our last cake. I put it in the box myself. "What's that cake doing there?" I didn't pretend for a moment that Evan wasn't up to something.

If he expected a cake brawl for old time's sake after I meticulously shined this kitchen, well, he knows me better than I know myself because I'd do it. In fact, I was one step ahead of him, sliding my talon toward it. I'd learned some hacks about cake brawls. The trick was to take all the ammo and attack first. As I slid in next to the cake, I was all hands, ready to sweep it up in one big chunk for some facetime. I quickly halted on my heel when I saw what was placed in the center of the cake. "Evan . . ." My voice decreased in volume so much it dropped into a whisper all the while the intonations increased in urgency.

"I know you don't have a problem digging into the center of a perfect cheesecake." He crossed the room, closing the gap between us.

"I do actually." I eyed the cake with the perfect princess cut solitaire diamond ring in the center, but my fingers trembled enough that I didn't want to touch it.

Evan was one step ahead of me, and carefully pinched the ring between his fingers, bringing it out of the cake without getting cake on it. It was obvious to me now; he had selected a cake without topping on purpose. He brought the ring close to his body, holding it protectively. He turned it over a few times and was so quiet, I thought he'd changed his mind. I ran my tongue along my lips, hydrating them, waiting for the best part but Evan didn't budge. This was the part he was supposed to get on one knee! Was he waiting for me to do it?

I wasn't ready for that!

I stared at his hands as they turned the ring over. When I gazed back at his face, he wasn't smiling. He'd clearly lost his nerve, or changed his mind, but I didn't want this to get anymore awkward and blurted out, "It's okay if you don't want to."

"What?" He blinked, nostrils flaring just enough to pin my feet to the ground. "Why would you think that?"

"It's just that you were hesitating—"

"Taking the moment in," He cut me off. "Wanting to remember this forever."

"Oh." I curtly made an actual O with my lips, feeling silly now, and threw out an excuse, "My nerves have been a wreck all day." Before I could ramble on about how I spent the whole morning slurping my coffee from the pot with ice and a loppy straw because I was hopelessly trying to do fun things to avoid the tears, he finally took a knee.

And I cinched every muscle I had in my body tight, holding everything in, so I wouldn't accidentally ruin *this*. I fought all day not to cry. I wasn't strong enough to handle this. Tears pricked at the back of my eyes, and I willingly blinked them down my cheek.

"I know we haven't talked about this much, but this month has been hard for me with all the changes. My parents moved. For a moment, I wondered if I should go, too. They are the only real family I have; I quickly stopped those thoughts when I realized I'd have to leave you. I was worried after you lost your job that maybe you'd want to move back to your family. That thought horrified me, too. I don't ever want to be away from you, and I realized we are each other's family. It's time we make it official because I don't want to imagine my life without you." He displayed the ring in his flattened palm. With his free hand he picked it up and held it out. "I love you, Jade. Will you marry me?"

"Yes." I squeaked out, but when I reached my finger out to receive my ring, yellow chicken feathers broke my tunnel vision. I giggled the sweetest giggle, already knowing this would be my best memory here at the bakery. "You had to do it when I was dressed as a giant chicken? Didn't you?" I managed to spread my fingers out and he finished slipping the ring on my finger while I added, "You couldn't tip me off to wear a nice dress or something? Can you imagine how this engagement selfie is going to look now?"

A rush of laughter fell from his lips, but I moved in to stifle it with a kiss. When I pulled back, I gazed down at my ring on my finger, fully taking it in. All the bad things that had happened to me led me to this moment. I wouldn't change any of it. "I love you, fiancé." I flashed the ring back at him, wiggling my fingers as I tried to get used to this engagement thing. I already know it would be the best thing to ever happen to me.

"I love you, too." Evan slipped his hand into mine, weaving his fingers perfectly through and we left our little bakery. Once outside, Evan rolled up the little tattered cloth Welcome rug for the last time. Unlike other nights where it was brought inside to be used again the next day, tonight he tucked it under his arm. "I'm keeping this for your next adventure, whatever that ends up being."

Suddenly I wasn't sad about losing the bakery. I had something much sweeter. I was beautiful, strong, brave, and now, *engaged.*

Thank you for reading Mingle All the Way!

Guess what? Jade's coworkers, Portia and Christian, are getting their own book. It's an enemies to lovers, slow burn, coming in Jan 2024. Available for preorder now. https://www.amazon.com/dp/B0CG2NRLJ7

Did you know Evan started as a side character in my Maid for My Billionaire Boss book. You can find his cameo here: https://www.amazon.com/dp/B0BSDSM3ST

Holidaze In Amesbury Excerpt

Charlotte

So, do I want to be in a serious relationship?" I nodded in answer to Nick' question, setting my seconds-after-another-friend's-perfect-wedding-mocktail glass down to clear my hands so I could better defend myself to my best friend, Nick. We were sitting near a window at the bar in Sterling Lodge, the *same* lodge where my three best friends held their destination weddings.

They all chose the town of Amesbury because, "it held the perfect winter wonderland background for a beautiful Christmas wedding." Amesbury was so secluded and charming it was named the number-one spot to have a Christmas wedding. I'd bought so many weekend packages to stay here as a bridesmaid, I was pretty sure I deserved a free upgraded bride package any day now—I just needed to find a groom.

"I do." My adrenaline ticked up—like way up—all the way up to my neck. I continued to use my hands to illustrate my point, something I always did when I got emotional. Placing my flattened palm on my chest to stifle the rush, I continued, "Do I want to go to vineyards and apple orchards?"

"—I love apple orchards," Nick cut in. "They have the best hard cider."

"Cheers to apple orchards!" I pinched the stem of my glass between my fingers, and tapped it with his, then lowered it to my lips so I could take another generous sip of my mocktail, made with their famous poinsettia infused tonic water. As I came up for air, I finished my sentence right where I had left off. "And hayrides with pumpkin spice lattes, sharing fluffy blankets that are perfectly coordinated to match our turtleneck sweaters, and do all the other insanely cute stuff?" I paused, but did not let him answer. He didn't need to tell me how he was feeling because I already knew. We were both tired of people acting as if I didn't know *all* our friends were marrying off at increasing speeds. That didn't sound like something I should be upset about, but no matter how much they insisted they would still make time for a night, one-by-one they disappeared into the baby-raising abyss.

I shifted in my seat, scooting closer to the edge. Sure, I'd get an invite to birthday parties, or a family picnic—and I enjoy supporting my friends in that way—but it was *painful* to always show up alone, when all I wanted was to be able to do what they were doing.

I saw all my friends getting married.

Of course, I saw them!

"I do," I rambled out. "I want all of that. But do I want to go on dates with every loser I barely know, just to suffer through hours of awkward conversations, only to find out he is a player like the rest of them?" I sealed my lips tightly and wagged my head back and forth.

No words are needed.

"I know what you mean." Nick leaned forward as he picked up my comment perfectly, like I knew he would. He always understood what I was going through. "I'm no Michelangelo's David but I want to find *one* woman who likes to cuddle on the couch, without having to twist her face into fourteen versions of duck lips so she can take the perfect ego-feeding selfie." He gestured toward me. "Is that too much to ask?"

"Oh, I hate selfies." I seethed, remembering his recollection of his last date. "When I'm on a date, I want to look at the other person, not stare at an isolated reflection of myself. I mean, I've been doing that long enough."

"Agreed!"

"Is it too much to ask my fairy Godmother to hurry and change a pumpkin into a carriage to transport me to the ball to meet my prince already?" I whined, but it came out forcefully like it was wrestling with a groan.

"Well, I hate to inform you." Nick rubbed his chin, cueing his transition to an armchair therapist, "nor do I want to be *that* guy who points this out, but you used your pumpkin in a latte for the hayride. I don't think you can ride in your pumpkin and drink it, too." His phone dinged, drawing his attention. "Uh, I'm sorry, Char. This is work." He placed the phone next to his ear, tacking on, "This will just be a second."

Grinning, I dropped my eyes back to my drink, rotating the glass slowly with my thumb and forefinger, wistfully dreaming of my prince. *What in the world was taking him so long?* I was at the stage in life, where I would be okay with backup prince number one—or even number two—if he had his act together.

I wasn't even sure if I believed in soulmates. At this point, I would be perfectly fine making a home with my soul neighbor—just as long as he didn't hog the covers at night, or listen to talk radio in the car. Well . . . technically, I could always bring earbuds. Maybe I could make an exception for the talk radio if he didn't complain about my bare feet being on the dash while I rode shotgun. *They always get too sweaty with shoes on!* They much preferred riding in the daylight.

Yeah, talk radio for a barefoot swap. That seemed like a logical compromise. Oh! And he'd have to listen to "Blue Christmas" by Elvis, on repeat, from Thanksgiving to Christmas, while also singing harmony, but he could totally have the other forty-eight weeks after that for his talk radio. Except for the obvious Elvis week where "Can't Help Falling in Love" would have to blast on all six speakers with the window rolled down to hear it outside of the car so we could dance under the stars—but that would be a given. If I had to explain dancing under the stars to any man, he definitely wasn't soul neighbor material.

Actually, since I'd been waiting so long, scratch everything except the dancing under the stars.

Dancing under the stars was a very reasonable condition that should be a cinch to finagle. Then, off to happily-ever-after land, and I wouldn't have to spend the rest of my life alone.

Nick set his phone screen down, leaning back into our conversation. "Sorry about that. Where were we?"

"I don't know," I started, ready to give up on love entirely so I could be finished dating. "Find me a dude who needs a maid but promises to take care of me forever—or something close—and I'd be happy to fill that role. I want to be done with dating." I pushed out my bottom lip and plopped my chin to rest in my palm. "It's such a waste of time."

Nick stretched one arm up and dropped it to scratch the back of his head. "I feel like I can put in another year, or two, tops, just to see if there are any stragglers who like to cuddle, but I'm going to end up where you are here shortly if all I get are duck lips."

"Another year and you'll be thirty," I commented, letting my eyes smack him with that reality.

"It's *adomania*." Nick's words came out soft, barely above a whisper, while he stared wide-eyed at me.

"Is that another word for a birthday?" I hiked a brow, letting a smile take over my face as I marveled at his rare talent for knowing the most unknown words that perfectly summed up every conversation. I called him the word whisperer. He hated that nickname, but that didn't stop him from going out of his way to find the most obscure words.

"Nah, not birthday." He blinked a couple of times as if he was trying to refocus on our conversation and then planted his gaze back on me. "It means your future is coming too quickly."

I let the definition ring over, and I had to admit he'd done it again. He'd summed up this entire conversation with one word. "It's perfect, 'adomania.'" My voice floated, as if it was still holding awe. He nodded gently, and I nodded back, our smiles synchronizing before I added, "Can you imagine how hard dating is going to be in our thirties?"

"I can imagine it will be pathetic—"

"So pathetic," I finished his thought like always. "Here we are, two amazing people,"—I straighten my spine, feeling an ego boost coming— "and nobody wants to spouse us up."

"Everyone must be blind." His words were laced with a low sputtering chuckle.

"Obviously." My eyes made a giant arc around the top of my lid as I strove for the most perfect eye roll ever. "I mean, look at you," I gestured to him with both hands. "You're like what? The most genius CPA on the planet?"

He shrugged only one shoulder, as if he were more-or-less accepting that as a compliment. "More like an office manager."

"Just call yourself a human calculator with all those skills." Exhausted from a full day of wedding party activities, and overly emotional, my words were starting to slur now, but I didn't care because I had a point to prove. I licked my lips, trying to remember what that point was . . . I wasn't sure, so I took another sip of my drink and stared at him until he came into focus. Then I remembered! "Oh, yeah, so what do you make a year, six figures?"

"Low six."

"Right!" I pointed at him accusingly because it would make him laugh. "You're rich!"

He snickered, as it was becoming obvious to both of us now that my "medication" was kicking in, but I continued as I still had a point to prove. I clumsily gestured at him again. "And you're buff! I've seen you with your shirt off, and you have two shadows of abs in there. Sometimes." My own laughter cut off my words as I giggled intensely and fondly looked back at my best friend. He was laughing, too. Not looking even slightly offended because he knew it was true.

Wrapping my fingers around the stem of my mocktail again, I lifted it to my lips and finished the rest, before setting it down, and seeing my glass was now empty. It was a little blurry, but I could mostly see it, and it was most definitely empty.

I was tired of being a glass-is-empty person. It was painful. Part of what one gets out of life is what they put into it. At some point, I would have to accept the plight I was given. It was then I made my decision. Letting out a sigh steeped in desperation, I put a voice to my decision, "If I'm not married—or at least engaged by Christmas—I'm forever giving up on dating—for eternity."

Nick quirked a skeptical brow. "This Christmas? That's eleven months."

"It seems like the only realistic thing to do. I could use all that time for a new hobby, or something." I pursed duck lips to remind him of his own fate, then tacked on, "Want to join me? We could make a pact."

"I don't know." He nervously scratched the back of his head. "I mean, I really like to cuddle."

I glared at him through my one good eye, which was less blurry than the other one. I picked up my glass to take another drink, but found it empty, which made me sad. I didn't want to be sad because I had a plan. Or more like a pact, and I was trying to snatch a partner for my pact. I flashed him more duck lips and said, "Quack," which sent us both into another rush of laughter.

"Okay," his voice sobered up, and he latched his eyes onto mine. "I'm done with duck lips. If I am not engaged by Christmas, I'll be done dating too, and we can do hayrides together."

"Wait." My eyes skirted the room, trying to see where that idea came from. "What did you say?"

"I said, I'm in. I agree with your pact. I'll give up if I'm not engaged by Christmas."

"No, no, no." I wagged my finger in the air. "What was that other part?"

"We can do hayrides together?" His voice teetered up, ending his statement as a question.

"Together?" I hiked a brow at him, feeling his vibes. "Are you saying, when we give up trying to find other people, we will just be together?"

"Well, I mean, if we are both single . . . it makes sense that we hang out, no?"

"Wait for a second. I'm getting an idea." I leaned forward, trying to pull him into my excitement. "If we aren't married by Christmas, then *we should get married to each other!"*

I could see him mouth the words "marry each other," but it wasn't audible. Then his eyes sprang wide as they hooked mine. "Yeah, that's the best idea ever!"

"I know!" I sprang to my feet, exclaiming, "I'm getting matching turtlenecks just in case! What's your size?"

"Large," he answered in a definitive tone and added, "I'll book the honeymoon suite here at the lodge—just in case."

"Right." I nodded, finding it perfectly acceptable. Then I leaned forward, extending a playful fist toward him. Somewhere over the years of wasting time together, we had accidentally made our secret handshake, and I was ready to deploy it. "Okay, Nick this is it. I swear if I'm not married by Christmas, I will meet you here in Amesbury, and marry you."

He balled his fist and pushed it out toward me for a bump, then we both made a half heart with our fingers and con-nected it in the middle. Nick didn't waste a second to confirm, "Deal."

Coming to Kindles November 7, 2023. https://www .amazon.com/dp/B0BRVQJWGC

Also By J.P. Sterling

Pardon My French Press (Coming Jan. 2024) https://
www.amazon.com/dp/B0CG2NRLJ7

About J.P.

Hey you! Thanks for being here.

Let me introduce myself.

I write wholesome stories and adore all things slapstick humor and heart strings.

Growing up, I binged on classic comedy like Lucille Ball, and Carol Burnette. It was a great escape from reality, even when the plots were farfetched. I discovered my love for writing slapstick comedy after motherhood and I haven't looked back.

Aside from writing, I'm also a wife and homeschooling mom, a holistic nutritionist, a jewelry designer, a professional archivist, former college instructor and lover of all things dark chocolate.

Author Clean Code: I like to make my stories about the story and not about a bunch of profanity, mature content, or graphic violence that are only there to shock you. I write my stories to be family friendly.

For free audio books please visit:

https://www.youtube.com/c/JpSterling

Find me on Instagram.

https://www.instagram.com/authorjpsterling/

Sign up to my free monthly newsletter to get the first look at my new books, free book offers and random updates.

https://landing.mailerlite.com/webforms/landing/q9c0v3